Dylan lifted Meggie onto the edge of the pool table

Then, stepping between her legs, he pulled her nearer, molding her body against his naked chest. She was so warm and soft, he couldn't get enough of her.

But her sweater was becoming a hindrance. Impatient to continue, Dylan reached down and grabbed the hem, then slowly tugged it up. Meggie met his gaze and the desire burning in her eyes startled him. With a soft sigh, she brushed his hands away and, in one quick motion, pulled off her sweater, then tossed it aside.

Dylan could barely breathe. She was the most beautiful thing he'd ever seen.

Meggie started shivering, and Dylan could see the indecision in her eyes. But just when he was about to call an end to this intimate exploration, Meggie reached out and slipped her fingers beneath the waistband of his jeans. Scooting back onto the pool table, she pulled him with her, until he was nearly lying on top of her.

"I'm not very good at this game," she murmured.

Dylan groaned. "Honey, if you were any better, the game would already be over...."

Dear Reader,

Who can pass by a fire station without hoping to catch a glimpse of the ultimate hero—the firefighter? I'm not sure about you, but I think those fire stations have more than their share of hunks in residence. So, when I started planning THE MIGHTY QUINNS miniseries, I decided it was time to turn one of those real-life heroes into a romantic one—Dylan Quinn.

Like all hunks, Dylan has left a trail of broken hearts behind him. In fact, my heroine, Meggie Flanagan, was one of Dylan's first casualties. So, years later, when he pulls her out of her smoky coffee shop and falls for her immediately, what's a girl to do but take advantage of the situation?

I hope you enjoy watching the second Mighty Quinn fall. Look for Brendan's story next month, the final book in THE MIGHTY QUINNS trilogy. And then visit my Web site at www.katehoffmann.com to learn about my first single-title release, *Reunited,* which features another Quinn sibling, available in June 2002.

Happy reading,

Kate Hoffmann

Books by Kate Hoffmann

Kate Hoffmann
THE MIGHTY QUINNS: DYLAN

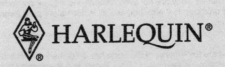

HARLEQUIN®

TORONTO • NEW YORK • LONDON
AMSTERDAM • PARIS • SYDNEY • HAMBURG
STOCKHOLM • ATHENS • TOKYO • MILAN • MADRID
PRAGUE • WARSAW • BUDAPEST • AUCKLAND

For Bunny

ISBN 0-373-25951-4

THE MIGHTY QUINNS: DYLAN

Prologue

THE WINTER'S SNOW had melted and a damp wind blew off the Atlantic, bringing the scent of the ocean into the South Boston neighborhood around Kilgore Street. Dylan Quinn climbed higher into the old tree, scrambling up branches that were just beginning to show their springtime buds, branches that could barely hold the weight of a squirrel much less an eleven-year-old boy. If he could just get a wee bit higher, maybe he could see the ocean from his perch. His da was due home today after almost three months away.

Winter was always a difficult time for the six Quinn boys. When the weather became too brutal in the North Atlantic, the swordfishing fleet drifted south, following the fish into warmer waters. And *The Mighty Quinn*, his father's boat, followed the fish wherever they went. With the coming of winter came the familiar fear that always grew in the pit of Dylan's stomach. Would Da remember to send them money for food? Would Conor be able to keep the family together? And would they all avoid the mistakes that might bring the social workers calling?

"Can ya see him?"

Dylan glanced down to find his younger brother Brendan standing beneath the leafless tree. He wore a tattered coat and his da's cast-off wool cap and his breath frosted in the air around his head. Like all the Quinns, he had nearly black hair and pale eyes that were an odd mixture of green and gold, strange enough to cause comment whenever they all appeared as one.

"Get away," Dylan yelled. Though he and Brendan were close in age, lately he'd come to resent his little brother's constant presence. After all, Dylan was eleven and Brendan was only ten. The kid didn't have to follow him everywhere he went, hanging on his every word.

"You're supposed to be watchin' Liam and the twins," Brendan said. "If Conor comes home and finds you out here, he'll eat the head off you!"

Their older brother, Con, had left the two of them in charge while he walked to a nearby market to buy food. They were down to their last dollars and if Da didn't come home today, Con would be forced to pinch whatever he could from the grocery to feed them for the weekend. They got breakfast and lunch at school, so it was easy to get through the week. But weekends were the worst—especially when the money ran out.

"Ah, shut your gob, you maggot," Dylan shouted, the ache of hunger acute in his stomach. He hated being hungry. It was the worst feeling in the world. When the pangs got too bad, he focused on his future, on a time when he'd be grown and living on his own. He'd have power over his own life then and the first thing he'd be sure of was that his cupboards would always be filled with food.

He saw the hurt in Brendan's eyes and immediately regretted his angry words. They'd always been the best of friends, but something inside Dylan had changed. Lately, he felt the need to distance himself, to rebel against the hand he'd been dealt. Maybe it would have been different if his mother had stayed. Maybe they'd be living in a nice warm house, wearing new clothes and having food on the table every night. But any dream of that ended six years ago, when Fiona Quinn left the house on Kilgore Street never to return again.

There were still traces of her to be found, in the lace curtains that now hung limply from the kitchen window and in the pretty rag rugs that she'd brought from their home in Ireland. Dylan really didn't remember much of Ireland. He'd only been four years old when they'd left. But Ireland was still thick in his father's voice, and he held on to that—maybe because it was the only thing he had of Seamus Quinn that he could hold on to.

But his mother was a different matter. He'd lie in bed at night and close his eyes and try to conjure a picture of her in his head, of her dark hair and pretty face. But the image was always faded and blurry and just out of reach. He remembered her voice though, the lilting sound of Ireland in her every word. He wanted to feel safe again, but Dylan knew that the only thing in the world that could make him feel that way was her. And she was gone—for good and forever.

"If you fall out of that tree and break your leg, you'll bring that witch from social services back down on us," Brendan called.

Dylan cursed beneath his breath, then slowly made his way down the tree. Usually Con was the one with all the common sense and Brendan was up for a bit of trouble. About ten feet above Brendan's head, Dylan swung from a branch and then dropped lightly to muddy ground beside him. With a playful growl, Dylan grabbed his brother in a headlock and rubbed his skull with his knuckles. "Don't give me any of your guff, boyo!"

They both raced toward the house and once inside, kicked off their muddy boots and shrugged out of their coats. In comparison to the damp outside, the house almost seemed warm, but Dylan knew that within a few minutes, the chill would begin to seep into his bones and he'd wrap himself in his coat again.

He wandered into the front parlor where Con had set up a small space heater. The floor was littered with blankets and pillows. The six of them slept here, together, for most of the winter. Dylan walked over to the heater and kicked away the sweater that Sean had so carelessly tossed aside. "Keep your stuff away from the heater," he shouted. "How many times do I have to tell you that? It'll start a fire and we'll all be burned to a crisp."

Dylan sat down in the center of the room and grabbed the stuffed bear that was Liam's favorite, then made it dance on the floor in front of his little brother. Brendan brought out a deck of cards and a box of stick matches and then dealt three hands of poker between him and the twins, Sean and Brian. Though it was nearly five o'clock, no one mentioned dinner.

It was better not to think about it and simply pray that Da would come soon, his pockets bulging with money.

The front door creaked and they all turned, each of them hoping to see Seamus Quinn enter. But it was Con who came in, holding a single grocery bag in his arms. Though he was only thirteen, in Dylan's eyes Conor was already a man. Tall and strong, he could best any boy his age and five years older on the neighborhood playgrounds. And no matter how bad things got, Con was always there, silent yet reassuring.

He glanced up at them then grinned against the hopeful looks sent his way. "Da will be home soon," he said. "And I've got dinner." He pulled a TV dinner from the bag. "Three for a dollar. There's spaghetti and fish sticks. Dylan, why don't you tell the boys a story, while I warm these."

"A story," Brian cried. "Tell us a Mighty Quinn story."

"Let Brendan tell," Dylan grumbled. "He's better at stories than I am."

"No," Conor said. "It's your turn. You're just as good at stories."

Grudgingly, Dylan settled himself on the floor. The twins wriggled closer and Liam crawled into his lap and looked up at him with wide eyes. Conor's stories always featured the supernatural—elves and trolls and gnomes and fairies. Brendan had a knack for stories of faraway places and magical kingdoms. Dylan's specialty was action, stories filled with deeds of derring-do—highwaymen who robbed from the rich and gave to the poor or brave knights who rescued fair maidens.

They had all played storyteller at one time to the younger boys, a trait inherited from their father. Seamus Quinn was always ready with a mythical tale of the Mighty Quinns, long-ago ancestors who followed only one rule—they never succumbed to the love of a woman. For Seamus Quinn believed that once a Mighty Quinn gave his heart away, his strength would leave him and he'd become weak and pitiful.

"This is the story of Odran Quinn and how he battled a giant to save the life of a beautiful princess," Dylan began.

Brendan flopped down on his stomach and cupped his chin in his hand, ready to listen. They'd all heard the tale many times before from their father, so Dylan knew they would correct any mistakes he made in the telling of it.

"You know the story of how Finn sent his son Odran Quinn to serve the great king of Tiranog. Odran was brave and loyal and the king wanted him to live in his kingdom and rule beside him. Tiranog was a paradise beneath the waves, where the trees were heavy with fruit and there was wine and food aplenty. The king sent his most beautiful daughter, the Princess Neve, to convince Odran to come. Of course, Odran didn't really like Neve, but he decided to go anyway, just to see what this fancy place, Tiranog, was all about."

"That's not the way it goes," Conor called from the kitchen.

"He fell in love with the Princess Neve. She was beautiful and she had a dowry of gold and silver," Brendan added.

"Well, he may have liked her a wee bit," Dylan said. "But he was careful not to love her."

"He said, 'Father, she is the most beautiful woman I have ever met,'" Brendan countered.

"All right, who's telling this story, you or me?"

"You!" Liam said.

"It was with a heavy heart that Odran left his father's home and rode away with the Princess Neve. They rode swiftly across the land and when they reached the sea, their white horses danced lightly over the waves. And then the sea parted and Odran Quinn found himself in a beautiful kingdom, full of sunshine and flowers and tall castles."

"When does the part about the giant come?" Liam asked.

Dylan gave him a playful hug. "Soon. On their long ride to the king's castle, Neve and Odran came upon a fortress. Odran asked Neve, 'Who lives in this place?' and Neve answered, 'A lady lives there. She was captured by a giant and he keeps her prisoner until she agrees to marry him.'" Dylan paused. "Odran Quinn looked up and saw the lady sitting by a window in the highest tower. A tear on her cheek glinted in the sunlight and Odran knew what he had to do. 'I must save her,' he said."

This was the part that Dylan liked the best, for when he told it, he pictured his mother as the lady sitting by the window. She was wearing a beautiful gown, all shiny and new, and her dark hair was braided and twisted elaborately around her head. And at her neck she wore a pendant, sparkling with emeralds and sapphires and rubies. His mother had a necklace like that and he remembered her rubbing it between her fingers when she looked worried.

"The giant's name was Fomor," Sean interrupted. "You forgot that part."

The image dissolved and Dylan turned back to his brothers. "And he was as tall as two houses with legs like huge oaks," he continued. "He carried a sword that was as sharp as a razor."

"Tell us about his hair," Brian pleaded.

Dylan lowered his voice and bent closer. "It was long and black and infested with spiders and weevils and his tangled beard nearly reached the ground." His brothers' eyes widened in fear. "And he had a big belly for every day he ate three little boys for lunch and three more for dinner. Bones and all." When they were properly terrified, Dylan sat back. "For days and days, they fought, the giant with his strength and mighty Odran Quinn with his cunning. And on the tenth day, when he was near death himself, Odran dealt the giant a mortal blow with his sword, and the giant came crashing down, the earth trembling all around. He was cold and dead as a stone."

Sean clapped. "And then Odran cuts his head off!"

"And then he climbs the castle wall and rescues the woman from the fortress and frees her from her prison," Brian added.

"That he does," Dylan said. "That he—"

The front door crashed open and they all turned to look. A moment later, Seamus Quinn strode in with a chilly gust of wind. "Where are my boys?" he shouted, his voice slurred. With joyous cries, Brian and Sean and Liam scrambled to their feet and went running toward their father, ending the tale of Odran and Fomor. Brendan and Dylan gave each other a long look, one laced with both relief and resignation. Though they were glad to see him, it was clear that Seamus had stopped for a pint or five before he'd come home. At least he'd come home.

"In all your stories, there's always a rescue," Brendan commented softly.

Dylan shrugged. "There's not," he replied. But he knew that wasn't true. With every story he told, he imagined himself as the Mighty Quinn, risking his life to save others, hailed as a hero by one and all. And the princess in need of rescuing always looked like his mother, or what he remembered his mother to look like. Dylan got to his feet, ready to greet his da. Someday he would be a hero. Someday, when he was all done growing and he could fend for himself, he would ride to the rescue and save those in trouble.

And maybe, against all his father's warnings, there would be a beautiful damsel who would thank him for his good deed by loving him forever.

1

THE ALARM SOUNDED at precisely 3:17 p.m. Dylan Quinn looked up from polishing the chrome fittings on Engine 22. He couldn't count the times he'd spit-shined the engine only to have the alarm sound. Most of the men of Ladder Company 14 and Engine Company 22 were upstairs relaxing after a long lunch but as they started to come down, Dylan tossed the polishing cloth aside and moved toward the alcove that held his boots, jacket and helmet.

A voice blared over the speaker system, the dispatcher repeating the address of the fire three times. The moment Dylan heard the address, he paused. Hell, it was just a few blocks from the station! As the others pulled on their gear, Dylan stepped out the wide garage doors and looked down Boylston Street.

He couldn't see any smoke. Hopefully, they'd arrive to find a contained fire that wasn't blazing out of control. The buildings in the older areas of Boston were built one right next to the other, and though firewalls prevented the spread of a blaze, the cramped spaces made it harder to get to a fire and then fight it.

The horn of the fire engine blared and Dylan slowly turned and gave Ken Carmichael, the driver, a wave. The truck pulled out of the station and as it passed, Dylan hopped on the rear running board and held on as they swung out onto the street. His heart started to beat a little quicker and his senses sharpened, as they did every time the company headed out to a fire.

As they wove through traffic on Boylston Street, he thought back to the moment he'd decided to become a firefighter. When he was a kid, he'd wanted to be a highwayman or a knight of the Round Table. But when he graduated from high school, neither one of those jobs were available. He wasn't interested in college. His older brother, Conor, had just started at the police academy, so Dylan had decided on the fire academy, a place that felt right the moment he walked in the door.

Unlike the days of his reckless youth when school barely mattered, Dylan had worked hard to be the top recruit in his class—the fastest, the strongest, the smartest, the bravest. The Boston Fire Department had a long and respected tradition, founded over three hundred years before as the nation's first paid municipal fire department. And now, Dylan Quinn, who had had the most rootless upbringing of all, was a part of that history. As a firefighter, he was known to be cautious yet fearless, aggressive yet compassionate, the kind of man trusted by all those who worked with him.

Only two other firefighters in the history of the department had made lieutenant faster than him and he was on track to make captain in a few more years, once he finished his degree at night school. But it wasn't about the glory or the excitement or even the beautiful women who seemed to flock around firefighters. It had always been about the opportunity to save someone's life, to snatch a complete stranger from the jaws of death and give them another chance. If that made him a hero, then Dylan wasn't sure why. It was just one of the perks of the job.

The engine slowly drew to a stop in the middle of traffic and Dylan grabbed his ax and hopped off. He double-checked the address, then noticed a wisp of pale gray smoke coming from the open door of a shop. A moment later, a slender woman with a soot-smudged face hurried out the front door.

"Thank God, you're here," she cried. "Hurry."

She ran back inside and Dylan took off after her. "Lady! Stop!" The last thing he needed was a civilian deliberately putting herself in harm's way. Although at first glance the fire didn't look dangerous, he'd learned to be wary of first impressions. The interior of the shop was filled with a hazy smoke, not much thicker than the cigarette smoke that hung over his father's pub after a busy Saturday night, but he knew a flare or an explosion could be just a second away. The acrid smell made his eyes sting and Dylan recognized the odor of burning rubber.

He found her behind a long counter, frantically beating at a small fire with a charred dish towel. Grabbing her arm, he pulled her back against him. "Lady, you have to leave. Let us take care of this before you get hurt."

"No!" she cried, trying to wriggle out of his arms. "We have to put it out before it does any damage."

Dylan glanced over his shoulder to see two members of his team enter, one of them carrying a fire extinguisher. "It looks like it's contained in this machine. Crack it open and look for the source," he ordered. Then he pulled the woman along beside him toward the door.

"Crack it open?" The woman dug in her heels, yanking them both to a stop.

Even beneath the light coating of soot, Dylan could see she was beautiful. She had hair the color of rich mahogany and it tumbled in soft waves around her shoulders. Her profile was perfect, every feature balanced from her green eyes to her straight nose to the sensuous shape of her wide mouth. He had to shake himself out of a careful study of her lips before he remembered the job at hand.

"Lady, if you don't leave right now, I'm going to have to carry you out," Dylan warned. He let his gaze rake her body, from the clinging sweater to the almost-too-short leather mini to the funky boots. "And considering the length of that skirt, you don't want me tossing you over my shoulder."

She seemed insulted by both his take-charge attitude and his comment on her wardrobe. Dylan studied her from beneath the brim of his helmet. Her eyes were bright with indignation and her breath came in quick gasps, making her breasts rise and fall in a tantalizing rhythm.

"This is my shop," she snapped. "And I'm not going to let you chop it apart with your axes!"

With a soft curse, Dylan did what he'd done hundreds of times before, both in practice and in reality. He bent down, grabbed her around the legs, then hoisted her over his shoulder. "I'll be back in a second," he called to his crew.

She kicked and screamed but Dylan barely noticed. Instead, his attention was diverted by the shapely backside nestled against his ear. He probably could have spent a little more time convincing her to leave the shop, but her stubborn attitude indicated that it would probably be a long fight. Besides, she was just a slip of a girl. He'd once carried a three-hundred-pound man down three flights. She weighed maybe one-twenty, tops.

When Dylan got her outside, he gently set her down next to one of the trucks, then tugged at the hem of her miniskirt to restore her dignity. She slapped at his hand as if he'd deliberately tried to molest her. His temper flared. "Stay here," he ordered through clenched teeth.

"No!" she said, making a move toward the door.

She slipped past him and Dylan raced after her, catching up a few steps inside the door of the shop. He grabbed her around the waist and pulled her back against him, her backside nestling into his lap in a way that made him forget all about the dangers of fire and focus on the dangers of a soft, feminine body.

They both watched as Artie Winton hooked his ax behind the smoking machine and yanked it onto the floor. Then he dragged it into the middle of the shop, raised the ax and brought it down. A few moments later, Jeff Reilly covered the mess of twisted stainless steel with a coating of foam from the extinguisher.

"This is the source," Jeff called. "It looks like that's all the farther it got."

"What was it?" Dylan asked.

Reilly squatted down to take a better look. "One of those frozen yogurt machines?"

"Nah," Winton said. "It's one of those fancy coffee-makers."

"It's an Espresso Master 8000 Deluxe."

Dylan glanced down to see the woman staring at the mess of stainless steel. A tear trickled down her cheek and she gnawed on her lower lip. Dylan cursed softly. If there was one thing he hated about fighting fires, it was the tears. Though he had given bad news to victims before, he'd never really known what to do about the tears. And to his ears, his words of sympathy always sounded so hollow and forced.

He cleared his throat. "I want you two to check around," he ordered as he patted the woman's shoulder. "Make sure we don't have any electrical shorts or hot spots in the walls. We don't know what kind of wiring they've got in here. Look for a breaker panel and see if it's flipped."

He pulled off his gloves and took the woman's hand in his, then gently pulled her toward the door. He should have been thinking about what to say, but instead he was fascinated by how delicate her fingers felt in his hand. "There's nothing you can do in here," he said softly. "We'll check everything out and if it's safe, you can go back in after the smoke clears."

When they got outside, he led her toward the back of the truck and gently pushed her down until she sat on the wide back bumper. A paramedic came rushing up but Dylan waved him off. Her tears came more freely now and Dylan felt his heart twist. He fought the impulse to gather her in his arms. She really didn't have much to cry about. All she'd lost was a coffeemaker.

"It's all right," he said. "I know you were scared, but you're fine. And you barely lost a thing."

She snapped her head up and leveled an angry glare at him. "That machine was worth fifteen thousand dollars! That's the best machine on the market. It makes four shots of espresso in fifteen seconds. And you and your ax-wielding Huns chopped it to bits."

Stunned by the intensity of her outburst, Dylan took a step back as if scorched by her words. She owed him at least a small bit of gratitude! "Listen, lady, I—"

"My name's not lady!" she cried.

"Well, whatever your name is, you should be happy," he said, unable to keep the anger from edging his voice. "No, you should be thrilled. Today was a good day. No one died." Dylan sighed, then lightened his tone. "You didn't get hurt, no one got hurt, you didn't lose precious family mementos or your favorite pet. You lost a coffeemaker, and a defective one at that."

Her mouth snapped shut and she looked up at him through thick, damp lashes. Dylan watched as another tear trickled down her cheek and he fought the temptation to reach out and catch it with his thumb.

"It's not just any coffeemaker," she reminded him.

"I know. It's an Espresso Deluxe 5000 whatever," he said. "A big hunk of stainless steel with a few gauges and a lot of tubing. Lady, I have to say that—"

"My name's not lady," she insisted. She brushed the hair from her face, then wiped off a smudge of soot from the end of her nose. "It's Meggie Flanagan."

Up until that very instant, the moment she'd said her name, Dylan hadn't recognized her. She'd changed—a lot. But there were still traces of the girl he knew so long ago. "Meggie Flanagan? Mary Margaret Flanagan? Tommy Flanagan's little sister."

She sent him a dismissive look. "Maybe."

Dylan chuckled, then pulled his hat off and ran his fingers through his hair. "Little Meggie Flanagan. So how's your brother? I haven't seen him for ages."

She regarded him suspiciously at first, then her gaze flitted over to the name tape on his jacket right below his left shoulder. Her expression fell and a blush rose on her cheeks, so intense Dylan could see it beneath the soot. "Quinn," she murmured. "Oh, God." She braced her elbows on her knees, then buried her face in her hands. "I should have figured you'd show up and try to ruin my life all over again."

"Ruin your life?" Dylan asked. "I saved your life!"

She jumped to her feet. "You did not," Meggie countered. "I was perfectly capable of putting out that fire on my own."

Dylan crossed his arms over his chest. "Then why did you call the fire department?" he inquired.

"I didn't," she muttered. "The alarm company did."

He grabbed the dish towel from her hand and waved it in her face. "And is this how you were planning to put it out?" Dylan shook his head. "I'll bet you don't even have a fire extinguisher inside, do you. If you only knew how many serious fires could be stopped with a simple fire extinguisher, I—" She tipped her chin up defiantly and his words died in his throat.

Meggie Flanagan. He almost felt embarrassed by his earlier attraction. After all, she was the little sister of one of his old buddies. There were unwritten rules between guys and one of the biggest was you didn't hit on a friend's sister. But Meggie wasn't that gawky kid with the braces and the goofy glasses anymore. And he hadn't seen Tommy for years. "I could cite you for a code violation."

"Oh, go ahead," she challenged. With a soft curse, she neatly turned on her heel and walked back toward the shop. "Considering our history, I wouldn't put it past you."

History? Dylan stared after her. "Meggie Flanagan," he repeated, this time out loud. He'd always remembered her as a shy and nervous kid, the kind of girl who stood back and watched the world from a safe distance. This woman could never be classified as shy. She used to be so skinny—and flat as a board. Even from his vantage point, he could see that she'd filled out in all the right places.

He'd spent hours after school at Tommy Flanagan's house, listening to music or playing video games. And she'd always been there, silently watching them through those thick glasses, standing in the shadows so she wouldn't be seen.

He'd practically lived at the Flanagan house when he was a senior, but it wasn't the video games that brought him back again and again. Tommy's mother was a cheerful and loving woman and she could always be depended on for an invitation to dinner, which Dylan gladly accepted.

Meggie always sat across from him at the table and whenever he'd looked up, she was always staring at him, the very same stare she fixed on him whenever they met in the hallways at school. She was two years behind him, a sophomore when he was a senior, and though they'd never shared a class, he saw her at least once or twice a day near his locker or in the lunch room. He'd seen how the kids poked fun of her and Tommy had been particularly protective, so Dylan had felt the same, considering her a surrogate little sister.

He watched now as she paced back and forth in front of her shop, rubbing her arms against the early November wind. The urge to protect was still there, but it was heavily laced with an undeniable attraction, an overwhelming need to touch her again just to see if his reaction was the same. Dylan shrugged off his jacket then walked over to her. "Here," he said. "You're going to catch a cold."

He didn't wait for her assent, merely draped the heavy waterproof jacket over her shoulders, allowing his hands to linger just a moment. The tingle that shot up his arms when he touched her did not go unnoticed. She stopped pacing and gave him a reluctant "thank you."

"What did you mean?" he asked, leaning back against the

brick facade of the building to watch her pace. "When you said I'd ruined your life once before?"

She frowned. "Nothing. It doesn't make a difference."

Dylan shook his head and smiled in an attempt to lighten her mood. "I hardly recognize you, Meggie. Except for the name. We never really knew each other, did we?"

An odd expression crossed her face and he wasn't sure if he read it right, through the soot and the windblown hair. Had he hurt her by his words? Was there a reason he was supposed to remember her?

To his disappointment, their conversation ended there. The radio on the truck sounded another alarm and the firefighters gathered at the scene stopped to listen. Dispatch gave an address in an industrial area, a factory fire, already a three-alarm blaze. "I have to go," he said, reaching out and giving her hand a squeeze. "It should be safe to go back inside now. And I'm sorry about your machine."

She opened her mouth, as if she had something more to say, then snapped it shut. "Thank you," she murmured.

He walked backward toward the truck, strangely unable to take his eyes away from her. For a moment, she looked like the girl he'd remembered, standing all alone on the sidewalk, unsure of herself, hands clutched in front of her. "Say 'hi' to Tommy the next time you see him."

"I will," she called, her gaze still fixed to his.

The truck rumbled to life behind him and Ken Carmichael honked the horn impatiently. "Maybe I'll see you around," Dylan added.

"Your jacket!" she called, slipping out of it.

He waved. "We've got extras in the truck."

He hopped inside the cab and took a spot behind the driver, then pulled the door shut. As they drove away from the scene, sirens wailing and lights blazing, Dylan glanced up and found Artie and Jeff grinning at him. "Gee, Quinn, what happened to your jacket?" Artie asked. "Did you lose it in the fire?"

Dylan shrugged.

"We could be fighting a fire on the moon and you'd still manage to find a woman to charm," Jeff said. He leaned forward and shouted to the driver. "Hey, Kenny, we have to go back. Quinn left his jacket behind again."

Carmichael chuckled, then yanked on the horn as he maneuvered through afternoon traffic. "That boy has a nasty habit of losing jackets. I'll just have to tell the chief to take it out of his pay."

Dylan pulled the extra jacket off the hook beside his head and slipped into it. This time he wasn't sure he wanted it back. Meggie Flanagan wasn't like the other women for whom the ploy had worked so well. For one thing, she didn't gaze up at him with an adoring look. From what he could tell, she pretty much hated him. And she certainly wasn't the kind of girl he could just seduce, then leave. She was the kid sister of a very old friend.

He drew a long breath, then let it out slowly. No, it would be a long time before he retrieved his jacket from Meggie Flanagan.

A THIN COAT OF GRIMY soot covered every surface in the shop. The grand opening of Cuppa Joe was scheduled for the day after Thanksgiving and Meggie was overwhelmed by the task in front of her. She still had to train eight new employees and finish up with the last details of the decor. A call to the insurance company assured her of a check for both a cleaning crew and a new machine. But she didn't have time to wait for the crew to come. Tables and chairs were due to be delivered tomorrow. If they expected to open on time, she and her business partner, Lana Richards, would have to get the place in shape on their own.

The smoke hadn't been the worst of yesterday's fire. The destruction of her espresso maker had been a crushing blow. "Three months," she muttered. "Three months until they can deliver another machine. I even offered to pay them extra for a rush order, but they said they couldn't do it. Every coffee shop wants one of those machines."

"Can you please stop with the machine?" Lana struggled to her feet and tossed a dirty rag into the bucket of warm water, then brushed her blond hair out of her eyes. "We'll just buy two Espresso Master 4000s. Or four Espresso Master 2000s. Anything so we don't have to talk about the espresso maker anymore."

In truth, she'd had to force herself to think about the machine. It kept her from lapsing into daydreams about the handsome firefighter who had ordered it destroyed. How many times over the past 24 hours had she caught herself adrift in a contemplation of Dylan Quinn? And how many times had the contemplation ended in a surge of well-remembered humiliation.

"This is our business," Meggie said softly. "We didn't spend the last five years saving every penny we made, working at jobs we hated, begging the Bank of Boston for a loan, just to have some overenthusiastic firefighter end it all with one swing of his ax."

Any woman might be fascinated by Dylan Quinn. After all, it wasn't every day you met a real life hero, tall and imposing in his firefighting gear. He seemed made for his job, dauntless and determined...strong and... Meggie sighed softly. There was probably a Dylan Quinn in every woman's life, a man who was the subject of an endless string of "what ifs."

What if she hadn't been such a geek in high school and he hadn't been such a god? What if she'd gotten her braces off a year earlier? What if she'd been able to talk to him without giggling uncontrollably? A moan slipped from her lips. Though she'd come a long way since those days, the memories were still acutely embarrassing.

Over the past years, she'd thought about Dylan Quinn every now and then, wondering what had happened to her first love. On lonely nights or after disastrous dates, she'd even conjure up a fantasy of what it might be like to meet him again. After all, she was different now. The braces and thick glasses had been replaced by perfect teeth and contact lenses. Her once lackluster hair color was now enhanced by one of Boston's best hairdressers. And most importantly of all, she'd grown curves in all the proper places.

Still, there were a few things that hadn't changed. She still wasn't very good with the opposite sex. Though she'd accomplished a lot in her professional life, her personal life left a lot to be desired. It probably had more to do with the men she chose to date, but Meggie just wrote her bad luck off as a lingering effect from too many years as a geek.

Dylan, on the other hand, had been one of the most popular boys in high school. With his dark and dangerous good looks and his devastating charm, he'd been every girl's dream date. But he'd still been a boy and her memories of him had always held an image of a tall, lanky, high-school Casanova with a killer smile. That image had shattered the moment she met those strange and beautiful eyes again.

All the Quinns had those eyes, gold mixed with green, a shade too unique to be called hazel. Those eyes that held the power to turn a girl's knees weak and make her pulse race. And to send Meggie right back to the pain and humiliation of that one night, the night of the Sophomore Frolic.

"The fire wasn't all bad," Lana said. "You got to see Dylan Quinn again."

"I needed that like a sharp stick in the eye," she said.

She and Lana had been friends since their college days at the University of Massachusetts, so there was very little that Lana didn't know about the men—or lack of them—in Meggie's life, both past and present. But the picture of Dylan Quinn she'd painted for her friend hadn't been very flattering—or entirely truthful. Had Lana been asked she probably would have described him as a cross between Hannibal Lector and Bigfoot.

The bell on the front door jingled and Meggie popped up from behind the counter, hoping that her new Espresso Master 4000 Ultra had arrived from the restaurant supply house. But it wasn't Eddie, the usual driver, who walked in the door. This man was tall and good-looking and...Meggie swallowed hard. This man was Dylan Quinn!

With a tiny groan, Meggie dropped back down behind the counter, then tugged on the leg of Lana's jeans. He was the last person she wanted to see! "It's him," she said.

Lana shook her leg until Meggie let go. "Who?"

"Dylan Quinn. Tell him to leave. Tell him we're not open. Tell him there's another coffee shop over on Newbury."

"Oh, my God," Lana murmured, staring toward the front of the shop, stunned by the revelation. "*That's* Dylan Quinn? But he doesn't look—"

Her words were stopped when Meggie slammed her fist down on Lana's big toe. Lana yelped in pain. "Get rid of him. Now!"

Her partner muttered a quiet threat, then stepped out from behind the counter. "Hello. I bet you're here looking for a good cup of coffee. Well, as you can see, we're not open yet. Our grand opening is in three weeks."

"Actually," he said. "I didn't come for coffee."

The warm rich sound of his voice seemed to seep into her bloodstream as Meggie cowered on the floor. She wondered what it might be like to listen to that voice for an hour or two. Would it become so addictive that she couldn't do without it?

"But I'm sure I could make something for one of Boston's finest," Lana continued. "We'll be one of the few places that serves Jamaican Blue Mountain. Would you like to try a cup? It's like nectar of the gods. An appropriate drink for you, I'd say."

Meggie groaned, then grabbed Lana's leg as she moved to the coffeemaker. "Don't serve him the Jamaican," she whispered. "It's the most expensive thing in the shop. Just get rid of him!"

Lana scooped some beans from a plastic container in the refrigerator, then dumped them in the grinder. "You're Dylan Quinn, aren't you?"

"Do I know you?" Dylan asked.

Just by the tone of his voice, Meggie could tell that he'd turned on the charm full force. And Lana, an accomplished flirt, was lapping it up like a sex kitten with a bowl of cream. He'd give her that boyish smile and those little crinkles at the corners of his eyes would make him look so appealing. And Lana would toss her perfect blond hair over her shoulder and laugh in that deep, throaty way she had. And before Meggie could stop them, they'd be rushing to the drugstore for a box of condoms.

"No," Lana said. "But I'm sure we can remedy that fact. I'm Lana Richards, Meggie's business partner. Meggie told me how you saved her life yesterday—and our shop. We're very grateful. Very. I hope there's a way I—I mean, we—can repay you."

Meggie cursed softly. Lana was doing this on purpose, teasing and taunting her, tweaking her jealousy until she'd be forced to stand up and show herself. Grudgingly, she stood up, then brushed her hair from her eyes. Dylan, who was now leaning over the counter, stepped back in surprise. "Meggie!"

She forced a smile. "I'm sorry, I was just…there was a thing I was…I had my head in the cooler and didn't hear you come in." She cleared her throat. "I'm afraid we're not open for business yet," she said, smoothing her hands over her jeans.

"The poor man has been fighting fires all day long. We could at least offer him something," Lana said.

Meggie crossed her arms beneath her breasts and watched Dylan warily. He'd changed out of his firefighting gear and now wore faded jeans, a T-shirt and a leather jacket, but he looked as rakish as ever. His hair, thick and dark, was still damp at the nape of his neck and she couldn't help but wonder how long ago he'd stepped out of the shower…wet…and naked.

She swallowed hard, then grabbed a rag and began to polish the copper-clad counter. "Gee, I would have thought you'd still be out pillaging," Meggie murmured.

Lana walked behind her and Meggie felt a sharp pain on the back of her arm as her partner pinched her. She cursed softly and rubbed her skin, then spun around and sent Lana a withering glare.

"Be nice," Lana whispered. "I'm going to do some book-work in the office."

"I don't have to be nice," Meggie muttered. "I detest the man."

"Then you go do the bookwork and let me be nice. He's gorgeous. And you know what they say about firefighters."

"What's that," Meggie murmured.

Lana leaned closer and whispered in her ear. "It's not the size of the hose, but where they point it that counts."

An unbidden giggle burst from Meggie's throat and she gave Lana a gentle shove toward the office. When they were finally alone, Meggie sent Dylan a sideways glance, then pulled a paper cup from beneath the counter and set it in front of him. He'd be getting this cup of coffee "to go."

He observed her intently as she waited for the coffee to dribble down into the tall carafe. A smile quirked the corners of his mouth, so easy and confident in his power over her. God, he was even more gorgeous than she remembered. All her friends in school had crushes on the New Kids On The Block, but Meggie had held out for the real thing—Dylan Quinn. Though he was two years older and a high school senior, she'd somehow deluded herself into believing that the feeling was mutual, that Dylan was in love with her. After all, every time he saw her, he'd smiled. And once or twice, he'd even called her by name.

And then it happened. Her brother, Tommy, had mentioned that Dylan was interested in taking her to her Sopho-more Folic. It was the first big dance of her high school career and she'd just assumed she'd be staying home like most of the other wallflowers in her class. But then, Dylan, the most handsome boy in all of South Boston High School, had agreed to escort her to the dance.

She could barely contain herself and she had told all her friends and they told all their friends until the entire sophomore class at Southie knew that Meggie Flanagan had a date with *the* Dylan Quinn. She'd bought a new dress and had shoes dyed to match. And when a corsage arrived earlier in the afternoon, she'd been so excited she'd nearly burst into tears. Then Dylan arrived, dressed in jeans and dragging his little brother, Brian, behind him. Brian, who was dressed in the tux and wearing a goofy grin.

At first, she hadn't understood, but then it became clear— Brian was her date, not Dylan. Though Brian was a Quinn, he hadn't really reached his full Adonis-like potential yet. He was still at least six inches shorter than she was and his idea of charm was staring at her dreamily while he tugged at his bowtie. She would have been better off going with her cousin or even her brother Tommy.

"I suppose you've come to apologize," she said, her back still to him.

He chuckled. "Actually, I came for my jacket. Remember?"

"Oh, right," she murmured. Of course, he wouldn't have come to see her. He was simply retrieving his gear. She slowly turned, then walked to the end of the counter. "I'll go get it. It's in the office."

"No hurry," he said. "You can give it back to me later. After I take you to dinner."

Meggie's heart stopped about the same time her feet did, and for a moment she couldn't breathe. Had she heard him right? Or was her mind playing tricks on her the same way it had all those years ago, when she'd convinced herself that Dylan Quinn harbored secret passions for her. "What?"

"Dinner," he said. "You look like you could use a break and it would give us a chance to catch up on old times."

Meggie swallowed hard. This wasn't happening, this couldn't be real. "I—I really can't," she murmured, turning away to busy herself wiping the back counter. "Not tonight."

"Then tomorrow night? I get off at eight. We could get a bite to eat, then maybe catch a movie."

She shook her head. She'd made a fool of herself once before, falling for him then having her heart stomped on. It wasn't going to happen again. She wouldn't allow it. "No," she said firmly. "I have too much work to do." Meggie grabbed his cup from the counter, then hurried over to fill it from the carafe.

When she'd finished, she spun around to hand it to him. But the hot coffee sloshed over the edge of the cup, scalding the top of her hand. She cried out in pain and dropped the cup, the hot liquid spattering over her shoes. In an instant, he was beside her, taking her hand gently in his and leading her to the small sink tucked beneath the counter.

Dylan flipped on the cold water, then held her hand beneath it. "Do you have ice?" he asked.

Meggie winced, then nodded at the icemaker nearby. He grabbed a towel then wrapped it around a handful of ice before returning to her side. "How does it feel," he asked.

"It hurts," Meggie replied. But in truth, she barely noticed the pain. It had vanished the moment he'd touched her, the flood of adrenaline simply washing it away. He touched her again, this time pulling her hand from beneath the water. He pressed her palm against his chest, then laid the ice over it. Beneath her fingers, she could feel his heart beating, strong and even.

She was thankful their roles weren't reversed for if he felt her heart racing, he'd know exactly how his touch had affected her. "That feels good."

He smiled down at her. "You should be more careful," he murmured, his gaze drifting lazily over her features. He stopped at her lips and she held her breath. For a moment, she was sure that if she closed her eyes and tipped her head up, he'd kiss her.

But then he chuckled softly, and pulled the ice from her hand. "Let see here," he said, carefully examining the skin just below her wrist. "It's a little red but no blistering. I think you'll be all right." He drew her hand up to his lips and pressed a cool kiss on her flaming skin.

Stunned, Meggie yanked her hand away as if she'd been burned all over again. He was teasing her, taking advantage of her nervousness when he was near. Dylan Quinn knew exactly how he made her feel and he was using it against her. "Please, don't do that," she murmured. She snatched the ice from his hands and drew a ragged breath. "I'll just go get your jacket and then you can be on your way."

Dylan stared at her for a long moment, then shrugged indifferently. "I'll get it another time," he said, stepping around the end of the counter. He looked back once. "I'll see you around, Meggie Flanagan." With that, he strode toward the door.

She fought the urge to run after him, to order him to stay away from her coffee shop and out of her life. But instead, all she could manage to do was admire the wide shoulders hidden beneath his leather jacket and the narrow hips accented by his jeans. He stepped through the door and a soft sigh slipped from her lips.

"I am such a coward," she murmured. She'd wanted to accept his invitation to dinner and she'd wanted his kiss to drift from her wrist, up her arm, to her mouth. She wasn't that same clumsy girl that she'd been thirteen years ago. She was a woman, now, almost thirty years old, and only occasionally clumsy. And most men even considered her pretty. She was smart and well-read and always felt that given the right man, she could be a sparkling conversationalist.

Yet the prospect of getting to know Dylan Quinn frightened her. Whenever he was near she reverted to that insecure and anxious teenager. Meggie groaned then pressed her forehead against the cool copper counter. If she'd only been able to think straight, maybe she could have done something once and for all, to even the score between them.

She imagined a wonderfully romantic dinner with witty

repartee. He'd fall madly in love with her in just one night and then she'd oh-so casually tell him that she wasn't really interested in a relationship. Or maybe she'd allow him to kiss her and he would experience an instant passion for her before she walked away.

Another groan slipped from her lips. This whole incident only proved one point. She was not the kind of woman who could handle a man like Dylan Quinn. So she had only one choice—she needed to stay as far away from him as possible.

2

DYLAN PARKED JUST down the block from Quinn's Pub. He let the Mustang idle, not sure he wanted to go inside. Saturday night was always a rollicking good time at Seamus Quinn's South Boston watering hole, with an Irish band and free corned-beef sandwiches. And there were sure to be plenty of beautiful women waiting inside, ready and willing to be charmed by one of the Quinn brothers.

How long had he gotten by on just charm alone? Since he was a kid, he'd used his winning personality and good looks to make a place for himself in the world, with his teachers, with his friends, with the opposite sex. Everyone loved Dylan Quinn. But no one ever got to know the real Dylan, the kid whose home life was in such chaos. They could never see how scared he was behind the smiles and the clever quips.

He wasn't scared anymore, yet he hadn't given up trying to charm every woman he met. But since Conor had fallen in love, Dylan realized that he wanted something more from life than just an endless string of beautiful women. He wanted something real and honest. Why couldn't *he* find a woman to love? And why couldn't a woman care enough about *him* to return that love?

"I probably should see a shrink," he muttered as he

reached over to flip off the ignition. A weaker man would make an appointment immediately, but he was a Quinn. Quinns just sucked it up and got on with their lives. If they had a problem, they didn't discuss it, they just fixed it. He shoved the car door open and stepped out into the chilly November night. Now, if he could only fix this strange attraction he had to Meggie Flanagan, he'd have all the answers he needed.

Dylan glanced both ways, then jogged across the street, following the sounds of a tin whistle and a fiddle and an Irish drum. After their first encounter, he'd written off any chance of a date with Meggie. Besides the fact that she held some grudge against him, she was still Tommy Flanagan's little sister. But after their second encounter, all the rules had been cast aside. The moment he'd touched her, something inside of him had changed. Though he'd tried, he couldn't think of her as anything but a sexy, desirable woman—who didn't want anything to do with him.

Maybe he was going through a phase. He'd had his fill of women who wanted him. Now, to avoid boredom, he'd become fascinated with the only woman in Boston who had ever rejected him, a woman completely immune to his charms. He shook his head. "You don't need a shrink, boyo, you just need a few pints of Guinness. That'll straighten you out."

He yanked the pub door open and immediately stepped into an atmosphere custom-designed to make him forget his problems with women. He took his time weaving through the crush of patrons and made a slow perusal of the room, searching for a pretty diversion, determined to forget Meggie Flanagan. Dylan started toward an empty stool at the middle of the bar, right next to a cute little brunette who was nursing a beer.

Sliding onto the stool, he waved at Sean and Brian who were taking their turns behind the bar. Seamus was shouting his way through a round of darts and Brendan stood nearby, chatting with one of their father's old friends. He glanced over his shoulder to find Liam at a booth with his current girl-friend. To round out the impromptu family reunion, Dylan was surprised to see Conor and Olivia sitting at the far end of the bar, deep in conversation, their heads close.

His big brother looked completely besotted and every now and then, Conor would pull Olivia near and kiss her without regard to the crowd around him. Had someone told him that Conor would be the first Quinn to fall prey to the love of a woman, Dylan would have laughed. Brendan or Liam were the more logical choices, the more tender-hearted of the bunch. But then, when it came to love, a guy never knew when it might lay him low.

Dylan looked across the room and watched his father en-gaged in a rousing argument over the exact position of a dart. They'd all heard the tales, the yarns Seamus Quinn spun about the Mighty Quinns and the dangers of love. Dylan had always wondered if he'd become the man he was in an effort to please his father—a guy who had never seemed to approve of anything Dylan did.

He hadn't been Conor, the son who kept the family together. And he hadn't been Brendan, the son who loved to work the lines on his father's swordfishing boat, *The Mighty Quinn*. And he certainly hadn't been Brian or Sean or Liam, the sons who adored their father without questioning his flaws. He'd been Dylan, the guy who could charm any woman, then walk away without a second thought.

But deep inside lived a person he'd rarely showed anyone—Dylan, the rebel, the kid who really didn't have a role in the family, the kid who blamed his father for the empty bellies and the endless insecurity. When his mother had been around, he'd felt safe. And after she'd left, he'd experienced the loss as deeply as if she'd ripped his heart from his chest and taken it with her. The man he'd become was all tied up in the past. He just hadn't been ready to untangle it yet.

Sean sauntered over with a pint of Guinness and Dylan cocked his head to the left. "Baby brother, why don't you buy this lovely lady a drink while you're at it." Though a free drink was always a good icebreaker, he really wasn't interested in conversation. The woman just looked a little lonely—a little vulnerable. The least he could do was to offer her a fresh beer while she waited for whatever or whomever she was waiting for.

The woman turned suddenly, as if surprised that he'd noticed her at all. For a moment, he was taken aback. A current of recognition shot through him and he tried to place her, to recall her name. But Dylan was certain that he'd never met her. He would have remembered because though she was pretty, she was also young, with a face that could only be described as...innocent. And those eyes, such an unusual shade. He would have remembered her eyes.

"What are you drinking?" Dylan asked sending her a warm smile.

She forced a smile in return, then stumbled off her stool. "I—I have to go," she murmured. "Thanks anyway." She grabbed her purse and her jacket, then hurried to the door, slipping out quietly.

Dylan turned back to Sean. "That makes me two for two today. I'm actually beginning to enjoy rejection."

"Don't beat yourself up," Sean said. "I've been trying to talk to her all night long but she'd have nothing of it. She just wanted to sit there, alone, sipping her beer and staring at me and Brian. You know, she looked familiar at first, but I'm pretty sure I don't know her."

"You, too? I thought I recognized her." Dylan shrugged, then grabbed his Guinness. He pushed off his stool. "If I'm going to spend the night crying in my beer, then I might as well do it with people who'll feel sorry for me." He wandered over to an empty spot next to Olivia, then sat down.

"Hey, Dylan," she said, her smile bright and affectionate. She leaned over and gave him a kiss on the cheek. "What have you been up to?"

In just a few short weeks, Olivia had become part of the family. Even though she and Conor weren't married yet, she was like a sister to him. Dylan liked having her around. After all, it was nice to get a woman's point of view every now and then. Growing up in a household of boys had its disadvantages.

"You look like you've had a rough day," Olivia said, draping her arm around his shoulders. "You want to talk?"

The offer was made facetiously for Olivia knew full well that the Quinns didn't talk about their problems. But maybe she'd be able to explain why he was attracted to the maddening and mercurial Meggie Flanagan, a woman who stumbled all over herself to stay away from him, a woman who hurled insults at him like fastballs in Fenway Park.

Had he suddenly developed a streak of masochism that only Meggie Flanagan could feed? Or was the notion of a woman playing hard to get so foreign to him that he found it irresistible? All he knew was that he couldn't stop thinking about her, recalling how soft her skin felt and how perfect her mouth was and how tempting her body looked.

"Well?" Olivia asked, interrupting his thoughts.

"Today?" Dylan asked. "Just the usual. Rescued a few kittens from trees, put out a few raging infernos, saved a few dozen lives. No big deal."

"And whose life have you saved lately?" Brendan slipped into the spot on the other side of Dylan and sent Olivia a warm smile.

"Mary Margaret Flanagan," Dylan said. Just the sound of her name on his lips brought back a flood of images. The sight of her face, covered in soot and marked with the tracks of her tears, then the fresh and natural beauty he discovered just an hour ago. Why couldn't he put her out of his head? There was just something so fascinating about her—the contrast between the girl she'd been and the woman she'd become.

Conor frowned. "Mary Margaret who?"

Sean leaned over the bar and chuckled. "Meggie Flanagan? Meggie Flanagan with the horn-rimmed glasses and the mouth full of metal?" He glanced over his shoulder toward the far end of the bar. "Hey, Brian, come here. Guess who Dylan saved."

"I didn't save her," Dylan insisted. "It was just a little fire. She's opening a coffee shop over on Boylston, not too far from the station. It looks like it'll be a real nice place. Anyway, yesterday afternoon her coffee machine shorted out and started a small fire. I had to carry her out when she refused to leave."

"You carried her out of her shop?" Conor asked.

Dylan took another long sip of his Guinness, then licked the foam from his upper lip and nodded. "Yeah, like a sack of potatoes. Although she wasn't nearly as lumpy."

"Oh-oh," Olivia warned. "That's how it starts."

Dylan's eyebrow rose. "What?"

Conor chuckled softly. "That's how Olivia and I met. I picked her up, tossed her over my shoulder and hauled her back inside the safehouse. Then she kicked me in the shin and called me a Neanderthal. After that, it was true love. That must be how it starts for us Quinns. We carry a woman away and that's the beginning of the end." He shrugged. "I guess I should have warned you."

"I'm not going to fall in love with Meggie Flanagan," Dylan insisted. "Carrying her out was part of the job, I had no choice. Besides, she hates me. She was downright hostile. She called me a Hun."

"Why?" Brendan asked. "You barely know her."

"But she knows you," Brian said. "At least by reputation. You cut a wide swath through the girls at South Boston High School. Was she one of the girls you left weeping in your wake?"

Why was that the quality that seemed to define Dylan Quinn? He wasn't remembered as a great athlete, which he was. He wasn't remembered as a loyal friend or a nice guy. It always came back to the women. "She was the kid sister of my best friend," Dylan muttered. "Even I have scruples. In fact, I was the one who got her a date to that sophomore dance. Didn't Sean take her?"

Brian shook his head. "No, that was me. And that was my very first date and probably the most traumatic experience with the opposite sex I've ever had."

"Oh, do tell," Olivia said, bracing her arms on the bar and leaning forward.

There was nothing a Quinn brother could refuse Olivia. Each one of them would jump into Boston Harbor in the dead of winter if that's what she asked. Recounting an embarrassing memory, complete with mythical Quinn embellishments, was nothing as long as it pleased her. "I was a foot shorter than Meggie and I had a pimple the size of Mount Vesuvius on my nose that night. I was so nervous I almost puked on her shoes. After that night, I didn't ask a girl out for two years."

"Do you think she's still mad about the pimple?" Dylan

asked. "Or did you do something stupid? Did you try to feel her—" He stopped, then gave Olivia an apologetic smile. "Did you try to get to first base with her?"

"Second base," Sean said. He pointed to his chest. "That's second base."

"I didn't touch her," Brian insisted.

"Why don't you just ask her why she doesn't like you?" Olivia suggested.

All the brothers looked at each other, then shook their heads. "That would involve a discussion of feelings," Brendan said. "It's part of Quinn family genetics that we avoid discussions like that. Haven't you read the manual?" He turned to Conor. "You have to give her the manual."

"Hell, it doesn't make a difference," Dylan said. "I'm not going to see her again, anyway."

But even as he said it, Dylan knew it was a lie. He had to see her again, had to figure out this strange and undeniable attraction he had to her. Maybe if he figured that out, he'd be able to unravel the rest of his feelings.

"I guess you're just going to have to wonder, then," Olivia said, giving his arm a squeeze. "But she must have a good reason. After all, how could any woman resist the charms of a Mighty Quinn?"

"YOU LOOK LIKE A girl who just found out her dress was caught in the back of her panty hose during the Grand March," Lana commented as she looked over Meggie's shoulder.

Meggie stared down at the photo from the Sophomore Frolic. She was dressed in a pouffy formal that looked like it was already out of style when she'd chosen it. But it was pink and shiny and at the time, it was the most beautiful gown she'd ever seen. She and her date stood beneath a flower-draped arbor. "At that moment, I would have rather walked the length of the gym with my dress up over my head," she murmured to Lana. "It was tragic. Humiliating. I thought I'd never be able to love another boy in my entire life."

"Your evening couldn't have been that bad. He's cute. A little short, but cute." She squinted at the photo, then reached over and scratched her nail on the surface. "What's that on his nose?"

"He wasn't Dylan," Meggie continued. "When they played our song that night, I thought I'd cry. 'Endless Love.'"

"See there," Lana said. "You two had a song. It couldn't have been that bad."

"It was *our* song—Dylan's and mine."

A frown wrinkled Lana's brow. "How could you and Dylan Quinn have a song? He barely knew you existed."

Meggie shoved the photo back into her purse and tossed her purse behind the counter. Then she grabbed a handful of pour spouts and began to shove them into the bottles of flavoring syrup. "Believe me, we had a whole relationship—in my poor deluded sophomore mind."

Lana slid onto a stool on the opposite side of the counter, then sipped at the latte she'd just prepared. "Sounds like you had it bad. No wonder you want revenge."

"Not revenge," Meggie said. "Just a little payback. Maybe then I wouldn't always wince when I think about high school. That whole thing followed me around until I graduated. I was defined by that night. I was the girl who carried the huge torch for Dylan Quinn, then got it dropped on her head. The geek and the god." She paused. "I've come a long way since then, but all it takes is one look at Dylan Quinn and I'm right back there, standing in the gymnasium with everyone staring at me."

It sounded like a good explanation for her attraction to Dylan—just a few residual feelings left over from that night so long ago. She was attracted to him because she hated him. After all, there was a thin line between love and hate, isn't that what people said? Or maybe seeing him again just threw her off.

She led such a well-ordered existence, focusing all her energies on the shop. Everything else, including her personal life, had its place and he was an anomaly. Even she knew a crazy attraction to Dylan Quinn didn't have any place in her life!

Lana shrugged. "Too bad you can't get him to fall in love with you. Then you could dump him and everything would be cool."

"*You* could do that," Meggie said. "You can wrap a man around your little finger and make him love every minute of it. And considering your strategical abilities, you'd go in with a battle plan that was sure to succeed." She grabbed a bottle of hazelnut syrup and turned the notion over and over in her brain as she twisted off the cap. If only she were more like Lana. More brazen with men, more uninhibited, more—

"We could do it," Lana murmured. "Why not? I mean, we put together a business plan for this place then convinced the bankers to finance it. If we use the same approach, we could make Dylan Quinn fall for you. We'll just use the same basic business and marketing principles we learned in b-school."

"How will that work?"

"We're selling a product—you. And we have to make the consumer—Dylan Quinn—want that product. Once he does, we'll just discontinue production and close the factory doors." Lana slipped off her stool, hurried around to the other side of the counter and rummaged around in a small drawer. She pulled out a battered old notebook where they kept a list of supplies they needed to order. She grabbed a pencil and drew a square at the top of an empty page. "This is our end goal. R-E-V-E-N-G-E."

"Not revenge," Meggie said, her interest piqued. She stepped to Lana's side. "That sounds so nasty. I'd rather call it...the careful restoration of the balance in my love life."

"We'll just call it revenge for short," Lana countered. "Now our intermediate goal is to get him to fall in love with you." She drew another box, then an arrow between the two. "Once that's accomplished, you can dump him and all will be right with the world."

"And just how do I make that happen?" Meggie asked. "You know what a disaster I am when it comes to men. As soon as I say something stupid or do something weird I get all flustered and they think I'm mentally unstable."

"You're exaggerating," Lana said. "You've just had bad luck with men."

"Do you have any little boxes and arrows to change my personality?"

"We won't need to change your personality," Lana said with a sly grin. "With my vast and detailed knowledge of the male ego, I could make Dylan fall in love with a parking meter if I wanted. Dylan Quinn is an unrepentant ladies' man. As such, he'll be quite easy to manipulate. All you have to do is play hard to get."

Meggie laughed. "I can barely get a date when I'm working at it. Why would he ask me out if I act uninterested?"

"Because you'll be a challenge and men like Dylan want what they can't have." She quickly wrote numbers down the side of the page. "Now, we'll have to develop guidelines. And you'll have to trust that I know what I'm talking about."

"I do," Meggie said. When it came to men, Lana definitely knew what she was doing. What Meggie didn't trust was her own feelings. Could she actually maintain her resolve and her objectivity around Dylan Quinn? She cursed silently. If she didn't do something, she was doomed to spend the next thirteen years as she had the last, reliving her mortification at the hands of Dylan Quinn, caught in the humiliation of a certified wallflower. "And I'll do whatever you say."

"There are few unbreakable rules regarding scheduling. First, there has to be at least four days between the time you accept a date and the time you go out on a date. If you accept a date for the same day, you'll appear too eager."

"All right," Meggie said. "What else?"

"When he calls, you have to wait at least a full day to call him back. And you can only call him once. If he's busy or he's not home, you don't call again."

Meggie nodded. This didn't seem difficult. It was all about what she couldn't do, not what she had to do. "Rule number three?" Meggie asked.

"On your first three dates, he can't pick you up at the house. You have to keep it casual. You'll meet him there, you'll be polite and gracious, and you'll call an end to the date at least an hour before you really want to."

She stepped back from the counter and frowned. "And this is supposed to make him fall in love with me? If I were him I'd slap me silly and leave with the next woman who walked out of the ladies' room."

"Think about it," Lana said. "This is the sex that invented the lost cause. Every man wants to be either a professional baseball player, a photographer for *Playboy* or the next lotto winner. Even if they can't hit a ball, operate a camera or don't bother to buy lottery tickets. It's part of their nature to want things they can't have."

"Is that it?"

"Then there are the kissing rules," Lana said. "No goodnight kiss on the first date, a kiss on the cheek for the second date, and lips, no tongue, on the third."

"He'll think I'm prissy," Meggie said.

"This is all basic economics, Meggie, supply and demand. The less you supply, the more he'll demand. You have to give him just enough to keep him coming back for more. He'll think you're mysterious and unattainable and he'll try even harder."

"This seems a little manipulative."

"Of course it's manipulative," Lana said. "The great thing is that men are so easy to manipulate."

"I'm not sure I can do that," Meggie murmured.

Lana scoffed then glanced around the shop. "Look around you. What we do at Cuppa Joe's is manipulative. We sell the best-smelling product on earth, we tempt people with special blends and fancy recipes. But basically we're selling them legal stimulants made with almost one-hundred-percent water at a seven-hundred-percent markup. When you have a good marketing plan, you can't go wrong."

Meggie considered the notion. It was a good plan and with any other woman, it might just work. But she'd never been a smooth operator with men. If she had to remember charts and diagrams and rules and regulations, she might just pass out from the effort. "It's too complicated," she said.

"We'll use my planning software to make a flowchart," Lana said. "Then you'll just have to remember one step at a time."

Meggie considered her options for a long moment. If she could pull this off, then she'd never have to think about Dylan Quinn again. And maybe she'd learn something. She hadn't had much luck with men up to this point. And the men in Lana's life seemed to multiply like rabbits. If anything, this was good practice. Why not just brush aside her reservations and go for it? "All right," she said.

Lana smiled and wrapped her arm around Meggie's shoulders, giving her a reassuring hug. "This will be fun. I'm bored with my own love life. It'll be interesting to run yours for a while. Now the only thing we have to do is pray that he stops in again. You're Catholic. Maybe you can go light a few candles."

"That's not what candles are for," Meggie said. "I can just call him and—"

"Nope," Lana said, shaking her head.

"I could walk past the firehouse and just casually—"

"Nope," Lana repeated.

"How is this going to work if he doesn't call me again?"

Lana sighed. "It won't work if he doesn't call you again. And it definitely won't work if you contact him first. So we just have to wait."

Just then, the phone rang and as Meggie studied the list of rules, Lana reached for the cordless. "Cuppa Joe's," she said. "The best beans in Boston."

Meggie listened distractedly until she heard her own name come up in Lana's conversation. Then she looked up and watched her partner chat amiably.

"Meggie isn't here," Lana said. She grinned and waved her hand, then pointed to the phone and mouthed something Meggie couldn't decipher. "Oh, I'm not sure when she'll be back. Should I have her call you?"

"Is that about the Espresso Master 8000 Deluxe?" Meggie whispered. "If that's Eddie, tell him I'm still willing to pay extra for a rush shipment."

Lana frowned and shook her head, pressing her finger over her lips to silence Meggie. "All right. I'll be sure to give her the message. Right. She'll get back to you as soon as she can." She hung up the phone, then took a deep breath.

"So?" Meggie asked. "Are they going to get us the 8000 or not?"

"Forget about that damn espresso machine! That was Dylan Quinn on the phone."

Stunned, Meggie pressed her hand to her chest. Her heart had already started to beat faster and for a moment she couldn't catch her breath. She cursed softly and tried to gain control over her cardiopulmonary system. "He called me?" First his visit last night and now a phone call. "What did he want?"

"He wanted to talk to you," Lana replied.

"But—but why didn't you—I was here!" Meggie cried. "Why did you take a message?"

Lana grabbed the notebook and waved it under her nose. "It's all part of the plan," she said.

Meggie crossed her arms beneath her breasts then stared at her partner for a long moment. Though the reasons seemed perfectly obvious to Lana, Meggie didn't have a clue. "If the goal is to get a date and I can't get that date unless Dylan Quinn calls, then why wouldn't you let me talk to him?"

"It's too soon," Lana said.

"So, I'll call him back in twenty-four hours, right?"

Lana considered that for a second, then shook her head. "No, I think we're going to play this a little differently. You'll wait for him to call two more times, then you'll call him back. That'll make him squirm a little."

Meggie couldn't imagine Dylan Quinn squirming under any circumstances. He just wasn't the squirming type. But if this plan had any chance of working, she'd have to trust Lana's instincts. And bury her own. Because Meggie knew that the moment Dylan showed any interest in her at all, she'd be lost to his charms. She pressed her palms down on the counter and drew a steadying breath.

She could make this happen—or she could make a complete fool out of herself by trying. Either way, her social life was about to become a lot more exciting than it had been in recent memory.

THE DAMP NOVEMBER chill that had hung over Boston for the past week had fled with the arrival of the sun. Dylan strolled along Boylston Street, staring into a bookshop window as he passed. He knew exactly where he was headed, but he wasn't ready to admit it to himself quite yet, so he slowed his pace and tried to focus on his window shopping.

All he was willing to admit was that he was in the area on his day off, picking up his paycheck from the station, and the day was so beautiful, he decided to take a walk.

Leaves skittered over the streets, pushed along by the warm breeze that blew from the south. It would have been a perfect day to head out on *The Mighty Quinn*. Brendan had called early that morning and wanted Dylan to help him ferry the boat up to Gloucester, but Dylan had other things on his mind.

He'd called Meggie three times in the past three days, but she hadn't returned a single call. Though he knew he ought to take the hint and forget her, he was starting to wonder if Olivia's advice might be right. Maybe he should just ask Meggie why she hated him so much. At least he'd have an answer and he'd be able to get on with his life. But pride had kept him from calling her a fourth time. Instead, he'd decided to pay her a visit.

When he reached the block of Boylston where Cuppa Joe was located, Dylan crossed the street, determined to observe the shop from a distance before venturing inside. And he was lucky he did, for he saw Meggie standing out in front of the shop in the sidewalk.

Two workmen stood on ladders, holding a sign between them as they struggled to hang it above the door. This would be the perfect time to talk to her, he mused. Her mind would be occupied with other things and he could just say his piece and get it over with. But Dylan hesitated, unable to step off the curb and cross the street.

"You're a right *eejit*," he muttered to himself, invoking one of his father's favorite put-downs in a thick Irish accent. "And you'll never learn when to leave well enough alone."

But in the end, he couldn't resist just one more chance to talk to her, one more opportunity to figure out why he couldn't get her out of his mind. Why all he could think about was touching her and breathing in the scent of her hair and gazing down into her pretty green eyes. He glanced both ways, then jogged across the street.

She didn't notice his approach, her back to him as she shouted directions at the workmen. He stood beside her and watched them work. "Nice sign," he finally said.

For a moment, he didn't think she heard him. But then Meggie slowly turned. From the look on her face, she wasn't very happy to see him. Her expression was one of thinly veiled apprehension. "Hi," she said, forcing a smile. "What are you doing here?"

Dylan shrugged, trying to appear nonchalant. "Nothing much. I had to stop by the station and I thought I'd do a little shopping."

"Here?"

"Yeah," he said, scrambling to make up a decent story. "Yeah, my brother Conor and his fiancée, Olivia Farrell, are getting married at the end of November and I thought I'd look for a wedding present." He glanced around. "Any suggestions?"

"There's a cooking store over on Newbury," she suggested. "You could get them a...blender. Or maybe some pots and pans." She shrugged. "Knives are always a nice present."

"Right," Dylan replied. "Knives."

The silence between them grew strained and he wondered whether he ought to just walk away and leave it at that. But he'd come this far. He reached out and grabbed her arm and turned her toward him. "Meggie, I—"

His words were interrupted by loud shouts and they both turned to see the workmen struggling with the heavy wooden sign. The breeze had caught it and they balanced precariously on the ladders, the sign swinging between them. But it was too heavy and an instant later, they were forced to let go.

Dylan barely had time to think. He grabbed Meggie around the waist, picked her up and shoved her toward the curb. But he wasn't quick enough to save himself. The sign crashed down, the corner grazing his forehead as it hit the ground and landed with a "whoof" between his feet and the shop.

He slowly shook his head, then turned to check on Meggie. She stood unharmed, her back pressed against a car parked at the curb, her eyes wide with shock. She blinked once, as if to bring herself back to reality. "You saved my life," she murmured.

He moved to stand in front of her, then skimmed his hands lightly over her face and her shoulders. "Are you all right? You're not hurt?"

She shook her head, gazing up at him. Relief washed over him and he took her face in his hands. "You're sure?" She nodded. And then, as if it were the most natural reaction in the world, Dylan leaned forward and pressed a kiss to her lips.

She moaned softly, but rather than draw away, he was caught by the feel of her mouth beneath his, soft, pliant, tempting. Hell, talking hadn't gotten him anywhere, so he had to resort to more blatant tactics. Dylan deepened the kiss, tracing a line between her lips with his tongue. She opened and he tasted, the blood rushing through his veins until he could hear his own heartbeat in his head. He'd never experienced such need from a simple, spontaneous kiss. The desire to continue kissing her was almost overwhelming, and if they hadn't been standing on Boylston Street with two workmen looking on, he might have kept on kissing her until neither one of them could stand.

Dylan hesitantly drew away, then stared down into her eyes, which were wider than they were when the sign had fallen. He drew his thumb along her lower lip, still damp from his kiss. "I'm sorry I pushed you, but I'm afraid if I hadn't you'd be underneath that sign right now."

"I know," she murmured. "Thank you. I guess I was lucky you were passing by."

"Actually, I wasn't just passing by. I wanted to talk to you and I was hoping you'd be here. I wanted to know why you hadn't returned my calls." Dylan prepared himself to accept all the standard answers. She was too busy, she was already involved, she was in the midst of moving and she didn't have a phone, she had to care for a sick aunt.

"I meant to call you back," Meggie said.

"You did?"

She nodded. "But, you see, if I had called you, you never would have walked by. And you never would have saved my life. So I guess it was a lucky thing."

Meggie rubbed her arms as if she were cold, but Dylan suspected it was a just a nervous reaction, as was her convoluted logic. The knowledge that he made her nervous gave him some hope. At least he wasn't making her angry. He reached out and placed his hands over hers. "The reason I called was that I wanted to ask, again, if you'd have dinner with me. I know we didn't get off to the best start, but I—"

"Yes," she blurted out, a blush staining her cheeks. "Yes, I'd love to have dinner with you. That would be great... wonderful. When?"

"How about tonight?" Dylan suggested.

Her smile faded slightly and she considered his suggestion for a long moment. "Could—could you just wait here a moment? I'll be right back."

Dylan watched her hurry up the steps to the front door of the shop. She disappeared inside and he wondered if she intended to come out again. She sure was an odd girl, that Meggie Flanagan, all nervous and fidgety, as if she were about to fall apart right in front of him.

He turned his attention to the two workmen who were now grinning at him in admiration. "Smooth," one of them said.

Putting on a stern expression, Dylan pointed to the sign still lying on the ground at his feet. "That's more than I can say for you two. You nearly killed her. Now, if you don't want me to call your boss, I'd get that sign up there and I'd make sure that it won't be coming down any time soon."

The pair did as they were told and by the time Meggie came back outside, they'd managed to attach the sign to the brackets. It was the perfect size and Dylan could see it would be visible up and down the street.

Meggie stood beside him and gazed up at the sign. "It looks good. I wasn't sure about the lettering and the colors, but I think everyone will be able to see it from a distance. And the coffee cup kind of says 'coffee shop,' so that helps."

"Yeah, it does," Dylan said. He turned to her. "So, is everything all right?"

"All right?"

"Yeah. Inside."

She smiled apologetically. "Oh, I just had to talk to Lana for a second. About the date—I mean, I didn't talk to her about our date. I just meant, regarding your invitation, tonight wouldn't be good."

"Then tomorrow night?" he asked.

"No, that wouldn't be good either."

Dylan reached down and caught her chin with his finger, then slowly tipped her gaze up until she met his. "Are you sure you want to go out with me at all?"

"Sunday would be perfect," she suggested, her eyes wide and unblinking.

"You want to go out on Sunday? Not Thursday, not Friday, not Saturday, but Sunday?"

"Yes," she said, nodding. "Sunday."

"All right, Sunday, then. How about I pick you up at seven? We'll have dinner at Boodle's."

"I'll meet you there," she said. "And six would probably be better." She hesitated. "And I'm really not a steak person.

How about Café Atlantis instead?" With that, she put on a bright expression, then pointed toward the shop. "I should go back inside. Lana needs my help."

Dylan nodded, then leaned forward to brush a quick kiss on her cheek, but whatever had possessed her to return his first kiss in full measure had disappeared. She deftly avoided him, skipping away and hurrying up the steps. Before she opened the door, she turned around and gave him a hesitant wave. "Café Atlantis, six, Sunday night," she called.

Dylan watched the door close behind her, then raked his fingers through his hair and cursed softly. He'd made a lot of dates in his life with a lot of different women. And they'd all expressed different levels of delight at the prospect. But this was the first time he'd asked a woman out and gotten the distinct feeling that this wasn't really a date at all. Sunday night? Six? At a place that specialized in sprouts and tofu?

Dylan sighed. Well, at least they had a date. That was a first step. And if he had to choke down textured vegetable protein instead of the best steak in Boston, then that's what he'd do. He figured as long as he was sitting across the table from the beautiful Meggie Flanagan, he'd be willing to eat cardboard and act like he enjoyed it.

3

MEGGIE JAMMED THE key into the door of her flat on the South End, then hurried inside. Lana trailed in after her, grumbling and complaining as she had all the way over.

"I still don't know why you need me here," she said. "We've got loads to do at the shop before we open. I have to proofread the take-out menus and the workmen want to put up the chalkboard menu tomorrow. And that second cash register still isn't working right."

Meggie kicked off her shoes, tossed her purse aside, and tugged her sweater over her head. "This was your plan," she said. "I just need to make sure I get everything right. I'm supposed to meet Dylan in an hour and it's going to take me fifteen minutes to get to the restaurant. I don't understand why I couldn't leave earlier. We were just sitting there drinking coffee for the past three hours."

Lana wandered into Meggie's kitchen and grabbed a bottle of juice from the refrigerator. "I kept you at the shop because I didn't want you to get crazy thinking about this date. And I'm glad I did. Look at yourself. You're a mess." She flopped down on the sofa. "Have you learned nothing?"

"It's not the date that's making me crazy," Meggie replied, brushing her hair out of her eyes. "I've had enough caffeine to keep me awake until next Tuesday." She unbuttoned her jeans and skimmed them down over her hips to her feet, then kicked them aside. She paused, staring down at her legs, her mouth agape. "Oh, no. I can't believe this."

"What?"

Meggie stuck her leg out in front of her. "I haven't shaved my legs in a month!"

"So what," Lana said with a shrug.

"I can't go out on a date with hairy legs."

Lana bent closer and studied the proffered leg. "Yes, you can. Hairy legs are the modern-day equivalent of a chastity belt. With those legs, you won't be hopping into bed with a man any time soon. Consider it a blessing."

"And what about my eyebrows? If I don't pluck, I'm going to look like Ernie. Or Bert. Or whichever Muppet it is that has that big eyebrow across his forehead." She moaned, then threw herself down beside Lana on the sofa. "This is no way to get ready for a date. I'm going to call and cancel."

Lana grabbed her hand and pulled her up, then dragged her to the bathroom. They stopped in front of the mirror above the sink. "Your eyebrows look fine. You're having a good hair day. Throw on a little blush and some lipstick, maybe some perfume and you'll be ready to go. Remember, don't take this too seriously. You're just having dinner and then you're going home. You don't even have to act like you're having fun."

Meggie grabbed her mascara, while Lana turned her attention to the closet, searching for an appropriate outfit for the evening ahead. As Meggie finished her left eye, she decided that Lana was probably right. A little mascara and some blush was enough for a date with—her hand shook and the mascara wand jabbed her eye. With a soft curse, she pressed her fingers against her eyelid to quell the burning. Both eyes began to water and by the time she was able to see again, her mascara was smudged to her cheekbones.

Lana tossed a dress into the bathroom. "That one is nice. Very flattering but not too sexy. And taupe is a neutral color. Red would be too obvious and black is too severe and any kind of pattern will distract from your natural beauty."

Meggie snatched the hanger from Lana, still rubbing her eye. "Maybe you should go on this date with me. You can hide under the table and do all the talking while I just move my lips."

Lana rolled her eyes in exasperation. "Just get dressed while I review everything you need to remember."

Meggie hurried out of the bathroom to grab fresh underwear from her dresser drawer. She decided if she couldn't shave her legs, then at least she'd wear decent underwear—and new panty hose. "We've reviewed this ten times already. I know it by heart. Maintain an air of mystery. Don't reveal too much. Avoid eye contact that lasts more than five seconds. Keep conversational topic light and irrelevant. And..." She knew there was one other point she was supposed to remember. She hurried back into the bathroom. "Don't drink any more coffee!"

Lana leaned into the bathroom, puckered her lips and made a loud smacking sound.

"Right," Meggie responded. "No kissing." She hadn't bothered to tell Lana about the kiss she and Dylan had already shared in front of the shop. It was a delicious memory she'd replayed over and over in her head.

At first, the feel of his mouth on hers had been a bit shocking. And then, after the initial surprise wore off, Meggie couldn't help but enjoy it, the warmth of his tongue, the taste of him. She'd never been kissed like that before. In retrospect, she really ought to put the whole thing out of her mind. It wouldn't do to get all caught up in the passion of that moment. But she couldn't help but relive it a few more times.

A faint buzzing sound filtered through the bathroom door and Meggie poked her head out. "Did you put something in the oven?"

Lana stumbled off the bed. "That's the front door. Probably one of your other admirers?" she asked in a teasing tone.

A withering glare was all she got in return from Meggie.

"I'll just go get it."

Meggie was glad to have a few moments to herself. She pulled the knit dress up over her hips, then slipped her arms into the sleeves. Then she closed the bathroom door and stared at herself in the full-length mirror. Lana was right. The color was perfect for a casual date. And the dress was flattering, clingy enough to show off her figure but not so tight as to make her look trashy.

"Maybe this won't be too bad," she said, snatching up the

package of panty hose. "After all, it's only dinner. I can handle that."

Meggie bunched up the panty hose in her fists, then tugged them over her feet. But the hose wouldn't stretch and she wrestled to get it up over her knees. Sitting down on the toilet to tug didn't help, so she waddled back into the bedroom and grabbed the bedpost. But a moment later, she felt herself losing her balance.

She tried to take a step but the tangled panty hose restricted her movement. With a cry of alarm, Meggie crashed into the dresser, then tumbled to the floor, her dress hiked up over her hips, her panty hose tangled around her ankles and a knot growing on her forehead.

Glancing up, she found Lana staring at her, her hands on her hips. "What are you doing?"

Meggie grunted as she kicked the panty hose off. "I'm trying to get dressed for my date." She cursed softly, rubbing her head. "Who was at the door?"

"Not was. Is," Lana said. "Dylan."

Meggie scrambled to her feet. "Dylan?"

"He decided to come and pick you up for your date, rather than meet you there." Lana reached out and tugged Meggie's skirt down. "Isn't that sweet? He's a real gentleman. Very considerate."

Meggie stumbled over to the door. Silently, she opened it, caught sight of the back of Dylan's head, then quickly shut the door. Even the back of his head was enough to set her pulse racing. "He's not supposed to come here! It's against the rules. You said I'm supposed to meet him there. What am I going to do now? The whole plan is messed up and we haven't even started yet."

"I don't think you have any choice. You can't very well tell him to leave. You'll just have to be gracious and acknowledge his thoughtfulness."

"That's easy for you to say. Your mascara isn't smudged so bad you look like a raccoon. You don't have that unibrow look going for you. And you don't have furry legs!" Meggie moaned, then leaned back against the door. "And I can't get my panty hose on straight."

Lana crossed the room, grabbed the wad of nylon, then re-adjusted the hose before Meggie stepped into them once again. "How does he look?" Meggie murmured as Lana tugged the panty hose up to her waist. "Is he gorgeous? Or just moderately hunky? If he's gorgeous I'm not going to be able to talk to him."

"Well, he doesn't have his panty hose in a twist if that's what you're asking." Lana grinned and sat back on her heels. "He looks great. He's obviously taking this date very seriously. He has on wool trousers and a really sexy sweater and a sport coat. Fashionable but still very masculine. If he weren't your guy, I'd be hanging all over him."

"He's not my guy," Meggie murmured as she glanced down at her dress. "Maybe I should change."

"You can do whatever you want," Lana said. She rose, then smoothed her hands over her thighs. "I'm leaving."

"Wait!" Meggie cried. "You can't go. We haven't reviewed everything."

"Good grief," Lana said. "You've been on a date before, Meggie. Just try to remember what we talked about and have fun—but not too much fun. Dazzle him." With that, Lana yanked open the bedroom door and stepped into the living room. Dylan turned as she walked past. "Meggie will be out in a second," she said.

Meggie slammed the bedroom door behind her, then scrambled to finish dressing. She wiped the mascara from beneath her eyes, dashed on a bit of lipstick, and tucked her flyaway hair behind her ears. As she held on to the doorknob, shoes in her other hand, she drew a deep breath, pasted a smile onto her face. "Be pleasant, easy on the eye contact and don't drool all over him the first time he smiles. I think I can remember that."

Never in her life had she been so nervous before a date. Maybe it was because she really didn't know how to handle herself since this wasn't really a date. It was more like a finely tuned military operation. But the moment she stepped into the living room, her heart began slamming in her chest and she felt as though all the oxygen had just been sucked out of the room.

Slowly, he stood and as she watched him, it was like one of those dreamy sequences in a bad movie. Everything went in slow motion. He turned and she was nearly blinded by the intensity of his smile and somewhere in the background she heard "Endless Love" playing. Meggie cursed inwardly, fighting the urge to retreat and regroup. How, in heaven's name, was she supposed maintain an air of mystery around this man? The moment he looked at her, she felt as if he could see straight through her, straight to the quivering mass of nerves and tangled panty hose she really was.

"Hi," she said, able to only manage one syllable at a time.

"Hi," he replied. His gaze raked the length of her body, then returned to her face. "You look beautiful."

Compliments. He made them with such sincerity that she almost believed what he said was true. Her mind raced for a reply. How would a woman of mystery respond? Meggie cursed inwardly. Forget the mystery, how was any woman supposed to respond with Dylan Quinn looking at her like that, like he wanted to undress her with his teeth? "Thanks," she said.

"I'm sorry to show up unannounced, but I live about a mile away. I figured it would be silly for us both to drive back downtown. The parking in Back Bay is always tricky."

Mystery, her mind screamed. "Is it? Oh, I hadn't noticed."

Dylan frowned. "But your shop is in Back Bay."

Meggie swallowed. So much for mystery. If it made her sound like a complete idiot, she'd have to abandon that plan. "I usually take the T." She hurried to the closet to get her coat, then shoved her arm into the sleeve. He was at her side in a mere second, taking it from her hands and holding it behind her. "Thank you," she murmured.

He smoothed his hands over her shoulders, his fingers warm through the soft cashmere. Manners were not a quality that she would have attached to the Quinn boys. When they were younger, they pretty much ran wild. But somewhere along the line, the rough edges had been smoothed. Meggie wondered whether the person responsible was one of the many women Dylan had known in his life, or if he'd grown into it himself.

"I'm glad we're doing this," he said, giving her shoulders a squeeze. "It will be nice to catch up."

Catch up on what? They'd never really spoken to each other in the past, beyond a quick hello at the Flanagan family dinner table. Perhaps he wanted to talk about how she used to hang around near his locker hoping to see him, or how she bought seven different lipsticks at the drugstore before she settled on the perfect shade of pink to match her Sophomore Frolic frock. Or maybe he wanted to discuss the seven thousand times she'd written out "Mrs. Dylan Quinn" and "Mary Margaret Quinn" and "Mrs. Meggie Quinn" on scraps of loose-leaf paper.

They could always discuss what she'd been doing with herself for the past three days, since he'd stopped by the shop and asked her on a date and kissed her right in the middle of the sidewalk. But then, that would take all of about one sentence. She'd spent her time thinking about Dylan Quinn— and wondering when she'd get to kiss him again.

"I'm looking forward to our dinner," she murmured. Meggie didn't realize what she said until after the words were out of her mouth. That wasn't right. She wasn't supposed to say that! "I mean, I'm hungry. Really famished."

Dylan grabbed the door and placed his palm in the small of her back as she stepped out. "Good. So am I."

As they walked down the stairs to the first floor, Meggie was glad he was behind her. He couldn't see the blush warming her cheeks or the way she chewed on her lower lip to steady her nerves. For all he knew, she was calm and composed and ready to enjoy a pleasant evening with an old friend.

Meggie drew a ragged breath. Now if she could only make herself feel that way, maybe she could get through the dinner with Dylan without making herself look like a certified lunatic.

"HERE, TRY THIS," Meggie said. "It's marinated bean curd. It has a very unusual taste."

Dylan wrinkled his nose and drew away, holding up his hand at the offered bite. "No thanks. I had my quota of curd for the day. I eat it for breakfast. Over my Wheaties. All the guys at the station do."

Meggie giggled then dropped the forkful of vegetarian stir-fry onto her plate. Dylan reached out for his wineglass and took a slow sip, studying her over the rim. All through dinner he couldn't keep his eyes off of her. There was something about her, a light that seemed to radiate from her shy smiles and her coy gazes. He'd been accustomed to women who were a bit more obvious about their desires. By now they'd have their foot in his lap beneath the table.

But Meggie was sweet and unassuming and sexy and alluring, a confusing jumble of contrasts. Dylan took a deep breath. She was real and so was the desire that raced through him every time he looked in her eyes. "This was good," he said, glancing down at his plate.

"You're just saying that," Meggie replied. "I know vegetarian probably isn't a favorite cuisine of yours. Not many men would have been adventurous enough to try it."

"It's not the food that's important," Dylan said. "It's the company." As soon as the words left his mouth, he wished he could take them back. He'd made a promise not to heap on the charm. But he always fell back on that when he wasn't sure what to do. She deserved better from him. "Would you like dessert?" he asked.

"I think there's a dessert menu." Meggie looked around for their waitress, but Dylan reached out and grabbed her hand.

"I had something different in mind than tofu cheesecake."

Her fingers were warm beneath his and he tried to remember how many times he'd touched her over the course of the evening. So many it had become almost an instinct, a quiet desire to feel her skin against his. He couldn't seem to stop himself and he wondered, after leaving her at her front door tonight, how long it would be before he wanted to touch her again.

But he wanted to do more than just touch her. She made it almost impossible to keep from thinking of other, more passionate alternatives. He'd stopped thinking of Meggie as a vulnerable little girl the moment he'd kissed her outside her coffee shop. She didn't kiss like a teenager, she responded to him like woman aching to taste more, a woman who was slowly wrapping him around her little finger.

Dylan turned and motioned to the waitress, and when she brought the check, he paid it and tossed a generous tip onto the table. Then he stood up and grabbed Meggie's hand, suddenly anxious to get out of the crowded restaurant. "Come on."

He helped her into her coat in the restaurant lobby, then rested his palm on the small of her back as he opened the door for her. The night was chilly and as they walked down the street she looped her arm through his. She started in the direction of the car, but he pulled her along in the opposite direction, until they reached an ice-cream shop about a block away.

"I wonder if they have meat ice cream," he teased. "Or hot steak sundaes with bacon sprinkles."

"All right, all right," Meggie said with a smile. "Next time, we'll go to Boodle's and you can have a steak."

"Deal," he murmured before he pulled open the door to the ice-cream shop. He was glad to know there would be a next time. Though he'd always been the one in control of the future of his relationships with women, he didn't feel that way with Meggie. With her, he couldn't assume anything.

They walked up to the counter and Meggie ordered a single-dip chocolate cone. Dylan chose a turtle sundae with all the trimmings. When their ice cream was ready, they took a seat at a small table near the window. As Meggie licked at the cone, she watched the pedestrians pass on the sidewalk. He watched her instead.

Meggie made eating an ice-cream cone the sexiest thing he'd ever seen—sexy because she didn't even realize what she was doing to him. Her tongue slid over the creamy chocolate and then she slowly licked her lips until they were damp and cool. A shiver skittered through him and he imagined what kissing her might taste like at this very moment. Or what her lips might feel like on his neck, or his chest, or his... Dylan fought the urge to brush aside everything on the table, grab her and taste her right then and there, the way he had that day in front of her shop.

He turned his attention back to his ice-cream sundae, pushing a cherry around the bowl with his spoon as he tried to stifle his thoughts.

"So tell me," she said, catching a drip of ice cream with her tongue. "Why did you become a fireman?"

Dylan shrugged. "When I was kid I wanted to be a highwayman. Or a knight of the Round Table." He glanced up. "But there's not much call for either in the Boston area."

"I guess not," Meggie said. "But why a fireman?"

"I always give the standard answer," he began. "I wanted to be a fireman because I could help people. But that's not really it. I think I just wanted to be worth something, to be known as someone who could be trusted when it really counted." His explanation stopped him short. He'd never said the words out loud, not even to himself. But with Meggie, he felt safe. She wasn't judging him. She'd known the boy he was and now she knew the man. "Plus, I knew I couldn't charm my way through the training. If I made it, it would be real."

"Are you ever afraid?" she asked, her gaze wide and direct.

"I don't think about being afraid, I just do my job. Besides, I think I was afraid enough when I was a kid that I've kind of developed an immunity to fear." He scooped up a spoonful of his ice cream and held it out to her. "Here, try some of mine. The caramel sauce is really good."

She leaned forward and ate the ice cream off his spoon then smiled. He was wrong. He was afraid of one thing. He was afraid he might make some stupid mistake with Meggie and she wouldn't want to see him again. He was afraid she'd see right through him and realize he wasn't the kind of man she wanted. "Why are we talking about me? Let's talk about something much more interesting."

"What?" Meggie asked.

"You," he suggested, a smile quirking the corners of his mouth.

"My life isn't very interesting. I went to college. UMass. I got a business degree and became an accountant."

"An accountant?" Dylan shook his head. He'd known she was smart in school, but the staid world of accounting didn't seem to fit Meggie—at least not the Meggie he was getting to know. Though she was quiet, he sensed there was a passionate woman beneath her calm facade, a woman who came out when he kissed her.

Meggie nodded. "It was a bad choice, but it was practical at the time. And it was good money and Lana and I were saving to open the coffee shop. We'd always talked about owning our own business, even back in college."

"Why a coffee shop?" Dylan asked.

"We wanted a place where people could come and relax. Where they could talk and read the paper and listen to music. Where they didn't have to watch the clock. Most of the coffee shops aren't really like that. They're more like fast-food restaurants. We wanted an atmosphere like the coffee shops of the fifties and sixties. We're going to have folk music and poetry readings in the evenings and on weekends. People won't just come for coffee, you'll see. It will have a real retro feel."

The excitement in her eyes was enough to make even Dylan interested in folk music and poetry. She knew what she wanted and she was going after it. And her determination to make it succeed intrigued him. No, this wasn't the Meggie Flanagan he knew as a kid. This was a passionate, determined woman.

Dylan pushed the remains of his sundae to the center of the table. He wanted to kiss Meggie more than he'd ever wanted to do anything in his life and he wanted to be alone with her when he did it. "All done?"

Meggie nodded and he took her hand as she got up from the table. He tucked her fingers in the crook of his arm and they walked out on the street. When they paused to look into a shop window, she caught him staring at her.

"What?" she murmured.

"You have ice cream on your face."

Meggie reached up, groaning softly, but Dylan caught her hand and pulled her into the shadows of a shop doorway. "Let me," he said. He bent close and rubbed his thumb over her lower lip. The contact was like a jolt of electricity, shocking but incredibly delicious. And when he licked the ice cream off his thumb, it was as intimate as if he'd kissed her. A sigh slipped from her throat and he didn't even think before he bent closer and did just that.

The instant their lips touched, he gently pulled her against him. She felt so small and delicate in his arms, soft and willing. At first her response was hesitant, but then she returned his kiss. A soft groan rumbled in his chest and he brought his hands to her face, molding her mouth to his. Dylan had kissed a lot of women in his life, but it had never felt like this, so intense.

Though desire raced through his blood, he knew that he wasn't kissing her to seduce her. He was simply kissing her to enjoy the sensation of her mouth beneath his, to savor the sweet taste of her. And when he finally drew back, he was satisfied that the kiss would be enough for now.

"I should get you home," he murmured, running his fingers along her cheek. "You've probably got a busy day tomorrow."

She blinked as if his suggestion took her by surprise. Perhaps she wanted to go on kissing him. But then, Dylan couldn't promise that after another he'd be able to stop. That was the thing about Meggie. When it came to her, he wasn't quite sure what to expect from himself. "Yes," she said. "I should be getting home."

He slipped his arm around her waist and they strolled silently down the sidewalk toward his car. Overall, he was pretty pleased with the way the night had gone. He'd convinced Meggie that he wasn't such a bad guy, he'd done enough to dispel her earlier low opinion of him and, considering her response to his kiss, there would be more dates in the future.

Dylan smiled to himself. Yep, this had been a good date as far as first dates went.

"IT WAS HORRIBLE," Meggie said. "It couldn't have been worse. With all that coffee we'd had, I had to go to the bathroom starting with the appetizers. But I couldn't remember if that fit into the flowchart or not. I was finally forced to excuse myself before they served the main course only to find out that I had a huge hunk of romaine caught between my teeth."

But in truth, it hadn't been horrible at all. It had been the best date she'd ever had. After her initial nervousness had abated, she and Dylan had thoroughly enjoyed themselves, talking and laughing and teasing as if they'd known each other for years—which they had. He'd seemed genuinely fascinated by everything she'd said and more than once during the night she caught him staring at her when he thought she wasn't looking.

Lana stared at her from across the counter at Cuppa Joe's. Meggie waited for the obligatory questions, expecting something resembling the Spanish Inquisition, complete with harsh lighting and torture devices. But surprisingly, Lana didn't press for more details.

"This plan will never work," Meggie murmured.

In truth, Meggie wasn't sure she wanted the plan to work. Dylan wasn't the man she thought he was. He was sweet and attentive and funny. He wasn't fickle and hurtful and thoughtless, like the boy she'd known in high school. No matter how hard she tried, she couldn't imagine that he'd do anything to deliberately hurt her—not now. Not after last night.

"Don't go all goofy on me," Lana said. "Just tell me, did he seem interested?"

Interested? If he wasn't interested, then that kiss they'd shared outside the ice-cream shop was an aberration. Or the kiss they'd shared in his car as he parked in front of her house. Or the kiss he'd given her at her front door. "I think he's interested."

"That's good. Did he try to kiss you?"

"No," Meggie murmured. Technically, she wasn't lying. He didn't try, he'd succeeded. And she'd been crazy enough to enjoy every moment of every kiss, from the tingling on her lips to the curling of her toes. She ran her fingers over her bottom lip, imagining that she could still feel the warmth he'd left there.

"He's nothing like the boy I remember," she said. The man he'd become was completely unexpected to her. There were many layers to Dylan Quinn and she'd just begun to discover them.

She'd known about his tough childhood. Though her parents had never talked about Tommy's best friend in her presence, she'd overheard their conversations many times. How Seamus Quinn drank too much and gambled too much, how the boys were left alone for weeks on end with a baby-sitter who was a bit too fond of vodka. But she'd always believed that they were only repeating rumors.

Now, as an adult, she could believe what her parents had said. There was something in his eyes, a wariness, that hinted he was hiding something, a vulnerability that he cloaked with a charming smile or a witty comment. The Dylan he showed the public and the man he really was were two very different people.

"Did he ask you out again?"

"Yes," Meggie murmured. "For Wednesday."

"And you accepted?"

She frowned. "Yes. Was I supposed to say no? That wasn't on the flowchart."

"That's only three days away, not four," Lana reminded her.

"Well, I didn't have a calculator along," Meggie countered. "I was trying to add it all in my head, twenty-four hours times four days. But then I wasn't sure if you meant four days on the calendar or 96 hours on the clock. I was confused, so I just said yes. Besides, he has Wednesday off. I had to take that into account."

"And did you end the date early?"

"I didn't have to," Meggie said. "After we had dessert, he

suggested that he take me home. He thought I'd probably have a busy day today."

Lana scowled. "Hmm. That's not good. He didn't ask to come in?"

"No," Meggie said. A sliver of worry shot through her. "What's wrong?"

"We may have to readjust the plan. I might have to replot this on the flowchart. This isn't ordinary behavior. Are you sure he enjoyed himself? Or did he have that anxious look that guys get when they wish they were someplace else?"

A sick feeling grew in Meggie's stomach. How was she supposed to know these things? Lana was the one with all the experience. The front door to the shop opened and they both turned to see a floral delivery man stride inside. Flowers and plants had been arriving in anticipation of the grand opening. A split leaf philodendron from her parents, an azalea in full bloom from her grandmother, a potted palm from the Boylston Street Business Association.

Lana pushed away from the counter, signed for the flowers, then grabbed the huge bouquet of Old English roses. "Who are they from?" Meggie asked as Lana set the vase on the counter.

Lana plucked the card out from amidst the pastel-colored blooms. Her partner read the card, then held it out under Meggie's nose. Meggie glanced down at the inscription and her heart skipped a beat.

I saw these flowers in the florist's window and they reminded me of you.

Dylan.

"They're from Dylan," Meggie said, a smile touching her lips. She leaned over and inhaled the scent, so much more intense than the traditional long-stemmed variety. The pastel colors of pink and peach and yellow immediately brightened her mood.

"They're beautiful," Lana commented. She sighed. "All right, I'll admit it. I really don't get this guy. He drops you off early without even an attempt at a good-night kiss, then he sends you flowers the next morning as if he just spent the most incredible night of his life. It doesn't make sense."

"What do you mean?" Meggie asked.

"Schizophrenia doesn't run in his family, does it?"

"Maybe we should just forget the plan," Meggie suggested. "It was all based on the fact that you knew the kind of guy Dylan was."

"No," Lana insisted. "We can make this work. I've just got to think about this. I want you to tell me everything that happened on your date. Spare no detail. This man is a challenge, but there's not a man on this planet that I can't figure out."

The fact that Lana wasn't really getting the whole picture was probably clouding her judgment, but Meggie wasn't about to tell her that she'd abandoned her carefully laid-out plan after just one look into Dylan's eyes. So she started at the beginning, leaving out the kisses. And as she relived every moment of her date with Dylan, she could understand why Lana found him such a puzzle.

One moment, she could swear that he was attracted to her and the next, she was certain he was just wielding his charm without even thinking. What made her believe she could possibly catch a man like Dylan Quinn? And even more crazy, what made her think she could let him go if and when she caught him?

"Can we talk about this later?" Meggie asked after recounting their dinner for the third time. "I've got other things to do. And you're supposed to drop off the proof for the take-out menus at the printers. We've got three days to decide how I'm supposed to act on our next date."

"All right," Lana said as she pushed away from the counter. "But I don't want you to give up on this. You need to even the score. You need to stand firm. It will all work out in the end."

Meggie nodded then headed back toward the office. But she couldn't stand firm. Every time Dylan Quinn looked at her she went from firm to mush in a matter of seconds. A look, a caress, a kiss, it didn't matter what. She just couldn't resist him. And if she couldn't resist him, then she'd get hurt in the end.

She found his jacket hanging on the back of the office door. Meggie picked it up and slipped it on, then wrapped her arms around herself. With her eyes closed, wearing the coat almost felt like his embrace. Memories of his mouth on hers drifted through her mind and her heart quickened.

Meggie opened her eyes and cursed softly. "I knew this would happen. One date and you're already mooning over him like some lovesick teenager!"

She slipped out of his jacket and into her own. If she waited until Dylan Quinn loved her before she dumped him, she wouldn't be able to dump him at all. Or maybe he'd dump her first. Meggie took a deep breath. He hadn't broken her heart yet. She could still get out with some measure of her pride.

Dylan Quinn had hurt her once. It was time to dump him and dump him fast—before he hurt her again.

4

DYLAN GRABBED THE hose and rinsed the rear bumper of the ladder truck. It was only then that he realized that he'd already washed that very same spot just a few minutes before. He sighed then shook his head. Luckily they hadn't been called out to any fires during his shift. His thoughts had been completely occupied with Meggie Flanagan from the moment he'd opened his eyes that morning.

He still hadn't figured out what it was that drew him to her. It had been ten days since he'd pulled her out of her shop kicking and screaming and as Conor had predicted, that one moment had caused a ripple through his life. Had she been any other woman, they would have rushed headlong into intimacy and already been on the downward slide of their short relationship by now. But with Meggie, the best was yet to come.

Dylan frowned, then snatched up a towel and began to wipe the water off the bumper. He wished he had known her better when she was younger. But maybe that wouldn't have helped. She wasn't the same girl he'd remembered. Somewhere along the line, she'd grown into a beautiful woman and the transformation was remarkable. But just as he carried the scars of his own childhood, she still held traces of the shy teenager she'd been, the girl who stood on the sidelines and watched, silent and unmoving.

"Quinn!"

Dylan peered around the back of the ladder truck. Artie Winton stood in the doorway, his arms hitched on his waist, a cagey grin on his face. "What?" Dylan asked.

"You have a visitor."

He stepped aside and an instant later, Meggie came around the corner of the truck. She was wrapped in a pretty cream-colored jacket that brought out her mahogany hair and green eyes, and her cheeks were pink from the chill in the air. And she clutched his own jacket in her hands. Dylan straightened and wiped his damp hands on his pants. "Meggie. What are you doing here?"

She glanced over her shoulder at Artie as she approached. "Is there some place we can talk?"

Dylan held out his hand and she placed her fingers into his palm. He led her toward the back of the firehouse, to a long bench. "Sit," he said. She did as she was told and he took a place beside her, refusing to let go of her hand.

"Thank you for the flowers," she said. "They're beautiful. And they smell heavenly."

He chuckled. "You're welcome. I enjoyed picking them out."

"You chose them yourself?" she asked as if the notion somehow surprised her.

"I did," he replied. Dylan groaned inwardly. If he thought they'd made any progress last night, he'd been wrong. Meggie was back to acting like a rabbit cornered by a wolf. She was skittish and wary and she could barely look him in the eye.

"I really shouldn't have come," she said. "I know it's against the rules but I had to talk to you."

"Rules?" Dylan asked.

She glanced up, her eyes wide. "I mean, the fire department rules."

Dylan grabbed his coat from her arms, then rose and pulled her up along with him. "Actually, we try very hard to maintain good relationships with the public so it's really not a problem if you visit. A lot of our time is just spent waiting anyway." He searched for an excuse to keep her there because she looked like she was about to bolt. "Why don't I show you around?"

"I just came to tell you something," she insisted. "And to return your—"

"Have you ever been in a firehouse?" Dylan asked.

She gave him a weak smile, then shrugged. "Not really. It's just that I—"

"Well, this is the pump truck," he interrupted, buying himself some time, "and that's the ladder truck. This one pumps water, the other has a ladder that we can use for access to taller buildings." He took her hand. "Would you like to sit inside?"

He helped her into the cab and then pulled himself up on the running board. Her fingers skimmed over the steering wheel and he remembered what her touch had done to him the night before, how soft and fleeting and addictive it had been. "This must be hell to parallel park," she murmured.

Dylan chuckled as he stepped down. "I don't have to drive, I just get to ride. And we pretty much get to park wherever we want." He reached up and grabbed her around the waist and then slowly lowered her to the floor. Her body slid along his, their hips making contact and sending a frisson of desire racing through his body. When she finally stood in front of him, he was tempted to kiss her right there, but he wagered a few of his co-workers were watching from the windows above.

"Maybe we should put my jacket away," he said. She followed him to the large alcove where the firefighters stowed their gear, and the moment they were out of sight of the windows, Dylan pulled her to him. He spun her around and she sank back into the jackets. With hands braced on either side of her head, he leaned forward and brushed a soft kiss on her lips, teasing then retreating, doing his best to lighten her somber mood.

How much longer could he go on like this, craving her kisses yet wanting so much more? He kept trying to think of her as that sweet vulnerable girl, hoping that might quell his desire, but that didn't work anymore. She was soft and she smelled nice and without a second thought, he could lose himself in a slow exploration of her body. "There," he murmured, smiling down at her. "That's much better."

"This has to be against the rules," she said, her eyes fixed on his mouth.

With a low groan, he captured her lips again, only this time with more intensity. The taste of her went right to his head, obliterating any thought of proper firefighter behavior. His tongue teased at hers, soft, persuasive, drawing her into the heat of the moment. And when her arms wrapped around his neck, he leaned into her, his hips pinning hers against the wall.

She was offering him more and he wasn't about to refuse. The passion they shared was unexpected and uncontrolled, a simple kiss the one thing that triggered it in full force. And though he knew he should resist, take things slow, nothing in her response gave him cause to.

His hands skimmed over her face then drifted down to her body. He pushed aside her coat and wrapped his arms around her waist. She went soft and pliant beneath his touch. The sweater she wore beneath her coat clung to her curves and he smoothed his palms over the soft cashmere as if he were touching bare skin.

And then he slipped his hands beneath the sweater and did touch bare skin, smooth, silken skin that felt like heaven against his callused palms. The blood roared in his head as desire threatened to overtake common sense. The ringing in his head was almost loud enough to drown out… Dylan froze, then slowly drew back. He stared down at Meggie, at her lips still damp from his kiss and at her face, flushed with desire and upturned to his.

"Meggie, I have to go."

"Go?" she asked, breathless.

The speaker overhead crackled and then dispatch came on with the address of an apartment fire. "We have go. There's a fire."

There was more than one fire to put out, he mused as he grabbed her hand. Dylan slipped into his jacket in an effort to hide the evidence of his own desire, then pulled her out of the alcove before the rest of the men reached the first floor. He casually leaned his arm against the panel of gauges on the pumper truck and pasted a smile on his face. "And that's how we get the incredible water pressure to fight fires here in Boston."

Meggie glanced around, her eyes going wide with the increasing activity, the men rushing around her, jostling her as they passed. Firefighters converged on their gear, grabbing jackets and slipping into boots. Dylan stole one more quick kiss. "What did you want to tell me?" he asked. "Tell me quick."

Meggie shook her head. "It's nothing. It can wait."

"Then I'll pick you up around lunchtime on Wednesday. Wear something warm," he called before hurrying to the alcove to grab his helmet and boots. Meggie stood in the middle of all the action as the crew made preparations to leave, a distraught expression on her face.

Then the trucks slowly pulled out of the station and Dylan hopped into the cab with the rest of his crew. "Thanks for bringing my jacket," he shouted over the sounds of the sirens.

She waved then slowly wandered through the open doors to the sidewalk. Dylan hung out the window and watched her as long as he could, until the engine was far down Boylston Street and she was just a figure in the distance. His mouth was still wet from her kiss and the scent of her perfume still swam in his head. He drew back inside, then smiled to himself.

"Hey, Quinn," Artie called from the seat beside him. "I see you got your old jacket back. You gonna leave it behind at this fire?"

Dylan shook his head and chuckled, smoothing his hands over the waterproof fabric. "Naw, that's a bad habit I'm going to break. I won't be leaving any more jackets behind from now on."

"WE'RE GOING ON a boat?" Meggie asked.

She stared at the huge boat that bumped gently against the dock. Though *The Mighty Quinn* looked like a perfectly seaworthy vessel, Meggie wasn't as certain of her own seaworthiness. "I've never been on a boat before," she murmured. "I mean, not on the ocean. I went rowing once on the Charles, but the boat tipped over and I fell in. We're not going on the ocean, are we?"

Dylan chuckled. "I suppose we could drag the boat up the interstate behind Liam's car, but I don't think that would be as easy as going on the ocean," he teased, giving a her a playful kiss on the cheek. "Besides, it's not technically the ocean, it's Massachusetts Bay."

"Why Gloucester?"

"Brendan's pulling the boat out for repairs during the winter and he knows a guy up there who has a boatyard, so he'll live up there for a while. He's working on a book about the North Atlantic swordfishing fleet and he wants to soak up the surroundings while he's writing it."

"I don't know anything about boats," Meggie murmured.

She glanced nervously between the car Dylan's brother had lent them and the boat. Meggie had fully intended to break off her relationship with Dylan today. She hadn't had the chance at the firehouse, but after another two days of careful contemplation, she'd convinced herself that putting Dylan Quinn out of her life would be for the best.

But she couldn't do it on a boat! What if he got angry? There was no place to run on a boat. Or what if he tried to convince her she was wrong? She couldn't avoid him on a boat. All he'd need to do is touch her the way he had at the fire station, his warm palms sliding over her skin, and she'd forget all her resolve.

She drew a ragged breath. A decision had to be made. Either she went back to Boston right now and put Dylan out of her life, or she spent the day bobbing around on the ocean with a man who had the capacity to erase all her doubts about him with just one kiss. Meggie winced inwardly. "Oh, what the hell," she murmured. What use was it resisting him? Why not just roll with the punches, let the chips fall where they may, and any other cliché that fit her situation. She could always break up with him tomorrow, or the next day, whenever she tired of the taste of his mouth on hers or the warmth of his hands on her body.

"My brother Brendan will do most of the work," Dylan explained. "Conor and I just have to help at the dock. And Conor's fiancée, Olivia, is coming along. We'll do the navigating so you have nothing to worry about. You'll have fun, I promise."

"You promise you won't get upset if I get sick?" Meggie asked.

"You won't," Dylan assured her, wrapping his arm around her shoulder. "The boat is pretty big and the water is calm today. And we won't be heading very far from shore." He turned to her. "We don't have to go if you don't want."

In truth, now that she'd decided to relax and take things as they came, she was looking forward to the day. Dylan had invited her to meet his brothers and he seemed so intent on having her along. And she couldn't ignore her own curiosity. She'd known *of* the Quinn boys in high school. Now she'd get a chance to know some of them personally—and maybe get to know Dylan a little better in the process. What harm could there be in that?

"Hey, Brendan! There's some bum loitering on your dock. You want me to throw him to the fishes?"

Meggie looked up and watched as a tall, dark-haired man hung over the side of the boat. He was as handsome as Dylan with those golden green eyes and that devilish grin. His gaze shifted to Meggie and she couldn't help but see the surprise register.

"And who's this?" he asked.

Dylan grabbed Meggie's hand and pulled her over toward

the crate that served as a step into the boat. "Meggie, this is my older brother, Conor. I don't know if you remember him. Con, this is Meggie Flanagan." He paused and Meggie knew he was scrambling for a word to describe what they were to each other. Girlfriend, acquaintance. "Tommy Flanagan's little sister," he finished.

Conor smiled warmly then reached out and helped her up on deck. "Glad to have you along," he said with a smile as disarming as Dylan's.

Dylan pointed up to the pilothouse where another Quinn stood in the doorway, as handsome and dangerous looking as the other two. "And that's Brendan."

Brendan gave Meggie a wave. He looked at her for a long moment, his eyebrow cocked up, then turned back to the business at hand. As if on cue, Conor jumped down onto the dock and a few seconds later, the engines rumbled to life. Like a finely tuned team, Dylan grabbed the bowlines and Conor the stern. At the last moment, they both jumped on board and the boat headed out of Hull harbor.

A pretty blonde came through the doorway to the main cabin and joined Conor, who introduced her as his fiancée, Olivia Farrell. Meggie had never been very good around strangers, but Olivia made her feel comfortable right away, taking her hand and leading her back through the doorway. The interior of the cabin was cozy and warm and clean, almost like a real house and nothing at all like she expected. "This is nice," Meggie commented.

"The bathroom is right down there," Olivia said. "The

boys call it the head, but I think that's such an awful word for it." She opened a picnic basket on the table. "I'm so glad you came along. I was wondering when we were going to meet you."

"Meet me?" Meggie said. She nervously clutched her hands in front of her, her fingers icy cold. The boat had already begun to sway and she had trouble keeping her balance. She quickly sat down at the table and gripped the edge with white-knuckled hands.

"The way Dylan talked about you at the pub the other night, it sounded like you two would be seeing each other again." Olivia began to pull deli containers out of the basket, potato salad, coleslaw, baked beans—each new selection making Meggie's stomach roil. Olivia handed her a chocolate chip cookie, then fetched a cup of coffee for them both. "He's such a great guy. I'm glad he's found someone."

Meggie took a sip of the coffee and it immediately calmed her stomach and warmed her hands. "He hasn't found me," she said, shaking her head. "I mean, we're not serious. We've only been out on one date. He's not really the type who gets serious."

Olivia glanced up, then smiled knowingly. "He's never brought a girl along on one of these trips. At least, that's what Conor claims. That must mean something, right?"

Meggie shrugged. "Maybe. But guys like Dylan don't fall in love. At least not forever."

"It sounds like you've been listening to too many of Seamus Quinn's Mighty Quinn stories."

"What are those?" Meggie asked, nibbling on the cookie.

Olivia sat down beside her and wrapped her hands around her steaming mug of coffee. "After their mother left, Seamus used to tell them these bedtime stories about their Mighty Quinn ancestors. The stories always contained the moral that to give in to a woman's love was a weakness. And the boys used to tell them over and over again when Seamus was out at sea. Brendan is the best storyteller, but I've heard Dylan spin a few tales, too." She sighed softly. "I can only imagine what their childhood was like without a single female influence in their lives."

Though Olivia was a virtual stranger, Meggie immediately felt at ease talking to her. "Dylan's never mentioned his mother. Do they see her?"

Olivia shook her head. "Never. Seamus told them she died in a car wreck a year after she walked out. Conor doesn't believe it. I'm not sure what Dylan thinks. He keeps his feelings pretty well hidden under all that charm. But sometimes I think he was the one most affected. Conor took over raising the family and Brendan helped his father on the boat. Dylan was kind of caught in the middle with nothing to do but become irresistible and irresponsible."

"He can be so charming," Meggie said with a soft laugh. "Sometimes I get caught up in it and I actually believe he has feelings for me."

Olivia met her gaze. "And what if he did? How do you feel about him?"

A smile broke across Meggie's face. "I've been in love with

Dylan Quinn since I was thirteen, since the first day he walked into our house with my brother, Tommy. He was so tall and so handsome, even back then, and I thought I'd die if he didn't love me back." She stopped suddenly, a blush warming her cheeks. "I shouldn't tell you this."

Olivia sat down next to her. "No. It's all right. The first time I saw Conor, I felt the same way, all fluttery and breathless, like a schoolgirl. There's something about the Quinn boys. They're so tough on the outside, yet so...vulnerable."

"Sometimes, I can't think straight when he looks at me. And when he kisses me I just—" Meggie stopped, certain she'd said too much. But when she glanced up at Olivia she found her smiling, as if they shared a wonderful secret.

"I know. I tried to resist, but it never worked. Maybe Seamus's tales have some truth to them. Maybe the Quinns have mystical powers."

Meggie nodded, then sighed. These were things she'd usually tell Lana, but that was impossible as long as Lana was focused on her plan. Besides, Olivia was in love with a Quinn. She knew what Meggie was going through. "Sometimes I believe I'm still in love with Dylan. And then I stop myself and try to keep from thinking about him like that. I know how he is."

"People change," Olivia said. "Sometimes the risks are worth the rewards." She rose, then pulled Meggie up with her. "It's a gorgeous day. Let's go up on deck."

They found Dylan and Conor up in the pilothouse with Brendan. The view from above the deck was spectacular.

Meggie looked out at the bay, then back to the shore, the skyline of Boston visible through a thin haze. But they were up so high, the motion of the boat was even more pronounced and she grabbed Dylan's arm to steady herself. She closed her eyes and drew a deep breath, praying that she wouldn't make a fool of herself and throw up the cookie she'd just eaten.

When she opened them, she saw Dylan staring at her. "Why don't we go down on deck," he said. "You'll feel better down there." He took her hand and helped her down the ladder. They walked around to the bow, then sat down on a gear locker. "How's that?" he asked.

"Better," Meggie replied, tipping her face up into the warm sun and breathing deeply until the nausea passed.

He slipped his arm around her shoulders and pulled her close. "Good."

They sat in silence for a long time, the both of them staring out at the water, breathing in the crisp air. Gulls hovered overhead, squawking loudly and diving for scraps that they thought all fishing boats offered. If only it could be like this all the time, Meggie mused. No doubts, no demands, just the two of them and the wind and the salt air.

She turned to Dylan, hesitated, then spoke. "I like your family. Your brothers are nice. And Olivia is wonderful."

"She is, isn't she. Conor is a lucky man. I'm kind of glad he was the one who proved the family legends wrong. A Mighty Quinn can be happy with a woman—the right woman."

Another silence grew between them and Meggie's mind raced. Was she the right woman? Or was she just another in a long line of "almosts"? There was so much she wanted to know, so many questions she needed answers for. "Dylan, why did you bring me along?" she blurted out.

He considered his reply for a long time, staring out at the horizon as if the answer was there. "I'm not sure," he finally said. "I just knew that once I got out on the water, I'd want you to be here with me. I wanted you to see this." He sent her a sideways glance. "It's part of who I am. If it weren't for this boat, I'd probably still be living in Ireland, a world away from who and what I am now. A world away from you." He glanced around, as if he'd said too much. "I hated this boat when I was a kid."

The vehemence in his words startled her and his cheerful expression had turned remote. "Why?"

He stood up and walked to the bow, then faced her. Meggie's breath stopped in her throat. Standing there, the wind in his hair, the sea at his back, he was about the most gorgeous thing she'd ever laid eyes on, like some ancient god risen up from the sea. He was wrong about the boat. He belonged here amidst the wide outdoors and the dark blue sea. Meggie pressed a hand to her chest, trying to keep her heart from racing out of control.

"This boat is why we came to America. It's what took my father away for weeks on end," Dylan explained. "This boat is what drove my mother to run out on us. This boat caused all the bad things that happened to me when I was a kid. Sometimes, I just wished it would sink to the bottom of the ocean so that we could have a normal family." He laughed bitterly. "But as I got older, I realized it wasn't the boat, it was what it represented. Loneliness, deprivation, fear."

His sudden honesty stunned her. Dylan must trust her very much to be so open about his childhood in her presence. What would Lana say about this? She'd have to revise her plan again. "What happened to your mother?" she asked, hoping that he'd keep talking.

Dylan shrugged. "I'm not sure. Conor used to believe that she was still alive, but I think we're all a little afraid to find out for sure. Afraid that this perfect image we have of her might not hold up in real life. All I know is that once she left, everything went bad." He smiled wanly. "My da and all his tales of the Mighty Quinns. All he had to do was look at his sons and see how much we needed her. That's why I used to hang out at your house. Your mom was always so nice to me. And she was a much better cook than Con."

"What if she showed up one day?" Meggie asked. "What would you do?"

He considered the question for a long time, his gaze fixed on her, the wind whipping at his hair. Meggie saw the pain in his eyes and suddenly, she was able to understand the boy he'd been, the boy who had used his charm to make a place for himself in the world, to protect himself from the terrors of real life.

Dylan slowly walked over to her and sat down. "I'd take her hand," he said, as he grabbed Meggie's fingers and curled them around his. "And I'd never let go again."

Her heart twisted. For a moment she wanted to believe that

he was talking about her. She leaned over and brushed a soft kiss across his lips. It was the first time she'd ever initiated a kiss. His eyes flickered and he looked surprised. Then he gave her a crooked smile and pressed his forehead against hers.

Suddenly, the barriers she'd built to protect herself from his charms completely dissolved. She didn't want to put this man out of her life, she wanted him to become a part of it. Yet everything between them was a tangle of secret motives and unresolved conflicts. She couldn't allow herself to love him, yet she couldn't seem to stop the feelings that surged inside of her.

Meggie drew a deep breath of the sea air and then kissed Dylan again, brushing aside her worries and doubts to simply enjoy the sensations that warmed her blood. She'd decide what to do later. For now, she wanted to believe that she could live in this fantasy world for just a little while longer.

"SO THAT'S Meggie Flanagan," Brendan murmured, staring down at the bow of the boat.

Dylan peered through the window of the pilothouse. Meggie and Olivia were sitting near the bow sipping at cups of hot cocoa and chatting amiably. He'd had his doubts about bringing her along. Meggie wasn't the type you just tossed into an unfamiliar setting. When she was nervous, she'd often retreat behind a wall of uneasy silence. But Olivia had made her feel welcome and Brendan had done his best to make the trip up to Gloucester smooth and uneventful. They'd docked late in the afternoon and Conor was out getting dinner for them all from a nearby tavern.

"That's certainly not the Meggie Flanagan I remember from high school," Brendan added. "She was only a year behind me, but I don't remember her having the potential to be quite so beautiful."

"She is beautiful, isn't she," Dylan said. "I mean not in that obvious, overblown way. She's real. Sometimes I think I could look at her for hours and never get bored."

Brendan clapped his hand on his brother's shoulder. "Conor said it. The minute you carried her out of that fire, you were lost."

"Maybe," Dylan said. "Maybe not. It's been almost two weeks since I carried her out of her shop. We've seen each other a handful of times. Just one official date though. And I still can't tell if she's interested."

"You can't blame her for being a little leery," Brendan said. "You are known to be quite the ladies' man, even among the six Quinn brothers."

Dylan winced. Why did that always have to come up? Why did his reputation seem to define who he was and how he'd behave? "I'm hoping to live that down sometime in the next decade. Meggie is the first woman I've really cared about. I don't want her to think I'm just marking time until another woman comes along."

"I suppose this doesn't bode well for me," Brendan said. "First Conor, then you. Da had a hard enough time accepting

Conor's engagement. He'll have a stroke when he hears about you. All those cautionary tales gone to waste."

"There's nothing to hear about," Dylan said. He gaze was still fixed on Meggie. She'd turned around and spotted him up in the pilothouse, then waved cheerfully.

"I see how you look at her," Brendan countered. "I'll tell you what I told Conor. Just don't screw this up. You may only get one chance to make it work."

Dylan nodded. He squinted against the slant of sunlight washing the deck. "I wonder what they're talking about?"

"You know women," Brendan said with a shrug. "They're probably comparing notes on the sexual prowess of the Quinn men."

"Really?" Dylan asked. "That's what they talk about? But they barely know each other."

"How the hell do I know? I know they don't talk about sports. And you can only talk about lipstick and nail polish for just so long. Sooner or later, I'd guess the topic might turn to men."

"I better get down there," Dylan said. "I don't want Olivia scaring her off."

Until now, he'd never really cared whether his family met one of his girlfriends. But Meggie wasn't a conquest and he wanted them to know her the way he did, to see how pretty she was and to understand why she made him laugh. And he wanted to prove to them that not all his relationships were shallow and short-term, that maybe, like Conor, he was capable of falling in love, too.

Not so long ago, the notion of love would have been unthinkable. But Dylan had seen what Olivia's love had given Conor. In just a few short weeks, Conor had left childhood wounds behind. He was complete, content, a man assured of a happy future. Olivia had given that to him and the more time Dylan spent with Meggie, the more he wanted to believe that she could make him happy in the same way.

After all the tales his father had told about the dangers of love, Dylan had never expected the emotion to touch him. But every moment he spent with Meggie brought him closer to the realization that it was possible to find the one perfect person to spend a lifetime with. Maybe she was the one.

He climbed down the ladder and as he came around to the bow, he ran into Olivia. She smiled at him then gave him a spontaneous hug. "Meggie is wonderful," she said. "Just don't do anything to mess it up, okay."

"Why does everyone think I'll mess it up?" he asked.

He found Meggie standing at the rail staring out at the harbor. He came up behind her and wrapped his arms around her, pulling her back against his body. "Aren't you cold?" he asked.

She nodded. "I was just about to come in and—" A fish flopped below her in the water and she jumped, then looked overboard. "What was that?"

Dylan rested his chin on her shoulder and saw the ripples. "I suppose it could have been a mermaid," he teased.

Meggie smiled. "There is no such thing. Except in Disney movies."

"Ah, but you're wrong," Dylan said. "Because my long-ago ancestor, Lorcan Quinn, he met a mermaid. And her name was Muriel."

"Then your ancestor Lorcan was as crazy as you," Meggie murmured, her gaze still fixed on the water, a tiny smile curling her lips.

Dylan had never been good at telling the stories, but he couldn't refuse the challenge of convincing Meggie. Besides, standing with her in his arms and the lights of the harbor twinkling off the twilight water, it was like magic. And it deserved a magical story. "Lorcan was a wild child," he began. "A very bold boy who was irresponsible to a fault. One day, he was *foostering* about and his da told him that he must make himself useful. So Lorcan offered to take the boat out and do some fishing. Well, he had no intention of catching fish. Lorcan lay down in the bottom of the boat for a wee nap. But he didn't sleep long. He opened his eyes to hear a lovely song filling the air. When he sat up, he found himself far from shore and drifting with a strong current."

"I can hear Ireland in your voice," Meggie said.

Dylan hadn't realized that he'd been telling the tale in the lilting accents of his homeland. But that's how the tales were supposed to sound, like music. That's the way they'd always told them when they were younger, in their father's voice. "Well, he looked over the side of the boat and he found a mermaid swimming about. Her name was Muriel and she lived in a kingdom at the bottom of the sea. She told Lorcan of the beauty of this kingdom and the riches that it held and she urged him to come with her. But Lorcan didn't trust her for he'd heard tales of how mermaids had lured fishermen to their deaths, so he grabbed his oars and rowed back to shore."

"So was she a bad mermaid or a good mermaid?" Meggie asked, turning her head to look up into his eyes.

"You'll see," Dylan replied, kissing her on the nose. "But Lorcan couldn't forget this mermaid. He heard her song every day as he drifted about in his boat. As he watched her swim around, he realized that he was in love with her, with her beauty and with the sound of her voice. But she was of the sea and he was of the land and there was no way they could be together. Still, this didn't stop him from coming out to see her, no matter what the weather.

"One day there was a great storm and Lorcan's little boat was caught by a tremendous wave. Muriel was there to save him but the storm was too powerful and it hurled them both against the rocks. As Muriel lay in Lorcan's arms, dying, she begged him to take her back to the sea, for only the sea could save her. Lorcan's love was strong, and though he knew it might mean his death, he jumped back into the raging ocean with Muriel in his arms."

"And did he die?" Meggie asked.

"Well, in the story that I always told, he met a cold and icy death in blackest depths of the sea and all because he was stupid enough to believe a mermaid."

"That's terrible," Meggie cried, giving him an elbow in the ribs.

"But in Brendan's version, Lorcan returns Muriel to her kingdom. Her father, who rules the ocean, is so happy to see his daughter again that he gives Lorcan a gift in return. He gives him the power to live underwater. So by sacrificing his own life for love, he's given a new life with Muriel and they lived happily beneath the sea—mermaid and merman—for the rest of their days."

"That's much better."

"When Da was away, Brendan always used to change the endings of the stories, until every story had six or seven different endings and we'd never know which one he'd tell. It kept them interesting." He paused. "I always thought Brendan's versions were a little sappy. But I like this one. You know, love conquers all."

He gently turned Meggie in his arms until she faced him. And then he bent closer and kissed her, slowly and deliberately, until his blood began to warm. How many times had he wondered what drew him to her? He'd spent countless hours trying to figure it out. Was it her beauty? Or her vulnerability? Or was it the past they'd shared?

As Dylan pulled her slender body against his and lost himself in the taste of her, he realized that it really didn't matter. They'd found each other. And for now, they were together. There would be plenty of time to sort out his feelings later— once he knew what they really were.

5

MEGGIE NESTLED INTO the curve of Dylan's arm then sighed. She'd been dozing since they'd left Gloucester, exhausted from the fresh air and the sea spray. She would have been content to stay exactly where she was, her head resting on Dylan's shoulder, snuggled beneath his jacket. But the lights passing by on the freeway told her they were nearing Boston.

It had been a near perfect day, warm for November with a blindingly blue sky. But it could have been pouring rain with ten-foot waves and she still wouldn't have believed it could get better. At first, she'd been a bit nervous about meeting Dylan's brothers. But they'd been as charming and attentive as he was and it wasn't long before she felt the last traces of her anxiety dissolve.

Part of that was due to Olivia Farrell. Meggie didn't have a sister, but when she imagined one for herself, she imagined someone just like Olivia. She was beautiful and sophisticated and funny and yet, she made Meggie feel as if they were the oldest and dearest of friends. With three Quinn brothers heaping on the charm, Meggie was lucky to have Olivia there to put them all back in their places. Both together and apart, the brothers had the uncanny knack of making a girl feel like she was the only woman in the world.

They'd parted with Olivia's promise to stop by the coffee shop on the day of the grand opening. And Meggie returned the promise with plans to visit Farrell Antiques as soon as she had a chance. But when Meggie waved goodbye from the dock, she knew there was every chance that she may never see Olivia Farrell again. The only connection between them was as fragile as her connection to Dylan Quinn.

Though she couldn't be sure what the future held, she was sure of one thing—making a place for Dylan Quinn in her future would be foolhardy at best. No matter how studiously she followed Lana's plan, one fact was still unavoidable. Men like Dylan didn't fall in love for keeps—maybe in romantic movies and dime-store novels, but not in real life.

But that didn't mean she couldn't enjoy what they had right here and now—just as she had today. Dwelling on the future only made the present more troubling. And she'd never really lived for the moment, tossing aside all her notions of propriety and leading with her heart instead of her head. For as long as she could remember, her life had been all planned out, studying hard in high school to get a scholarship, studying hard in college to get a good job, working hard at her job to save for the coffee shop.

Now all her professional dreams were about to come true, why couldn't she make a few of her personal fantasies happen at the same time, before the opportunity slipped through her fingers? Her thirtieth birthday was right around the corner. She'd at least like to experience mind-bending, toe-curling passion before she passed that milestone, the kind of passion that usually came with a brief and completely inappropriate affair with an unattainable man. And if that's what she wanted, then Dylan Quinn fit the bill.

"Are we home yet?" she murmured, straightening to look at him.

His face was illuminated by the lights from the dashboard and the passing streetlights and for a moment her breath caught in her throat. There were moments when she wished she could stop time so she could look at him, so she could memorize every plane and angle of his face and examine the strong line of his jaw and the sculpted shape of his mouth.

"I have to stop by the pub," Dylan said. "I promised Brian and Sean I'd take the deposit to the bank on my way home." He wove his hand through the hair at her nape and a delicious shiver skittered down her spine. "I know you're tired, but it will just be a few minutes."

She wrapped his jacket around herself, suddenly wide awake. "I had a nice time today," she said.

"Me, too."

They pulled up in front of the pub a few moments later. Dylan glanced at his watch then at the darkened exterior of Quinn's Pub. "I see Sean and Brian didn't bother to stick around. Closing time is at 2:00 a.m. and it's 2:05 right now." He turned off the ignition, then bent closer to Meggie and brushed a soft kiss across her lips. "I just have to run inside. And you have to come with me. I don't want you waiting out here alone."

Meggie straightened in her seat then stretched sinuously. "All right," she said, handing him his jacket.

Dylan hopped out of the Mustang and jogged around to her side, then helped her out of the car. They crossed the street, hand in hand, and he unlocked the front door of the pub and let her step inside first. Reaching around her, he flipped on the lights. Neon sputtered to life and bright light bounced off the wide mirror behind the bar. The smell of spilled beer and stale cigarette smoke was an assault to the senses after a day on the water, but Meggie ignored it in favor of her curiosity. So this was where Dylan spent his free time. And this is where he'd obviously met his share of beautiful women.

"I've never really been to a bar before," Meggie murmured.

"What?" Dylan asked as he tossed his jacket over the bar.

Meggie knew he'd heard her. He just couldn't believe her. "I know what they look like. I've seen *Cheers*. But in college I spent my Friday and Saturday nights studying. And after I started working, I just didn't have the time. Besides, they're always so crowded. Too many strangers."

"So where do you meet men?" Dylan asked.

A blush warmed her cheeks. So much for honesty. "That must be my problem. They all hang out at bars, don't they. And here I've been spending my free time at pottery class hoping to meet the man of my dreams."

Dylan chuckled and Meggie forced a smile, relieved that she'd deflected his question so adeptly. She stared down at the floor and pushed a scrap of paper around with her shoe. "There really haven't been that many men in my life," she murmured. "I suppose I shouldn't admit that, but it's the truth."

Dylan hooked a finger beneath her chin and tipped her gaze back up to his. "I can tell you right now," he said. "If you walked into this bar on a Friday night, you'd have men lined up on either side of you in just a few minutes."

She couldn't help but warm beneath his compliment. He always made her feel so special. But then that was all part of his charm, wasn't it. "The next time I want to meet a nice guy, I'll just set my house on fire."

He laughed, then grabbed her hand and pulled her toward the bar. When he settled her on a stool, he helped her out of her jacket. "Meeting a man in a bar isn't so tough. It's worse for the guy. He risks rejection in front of all his buddies. That's enough to scare any man off. All a woman has to do is look pretty."

"That can't be all it takes."

"Here, I'll show you." He stepped around the end of the bar and grabbed a bottle of rum. One after another, he added liquor and fruit juice to a glass of ice, then finished it with a drizzle of red syrup and dropped in a cherry and a chunk of pineapple. He set it in front of her.

"What's this?" she asked.

"That's a rum punch. They're popular in the tropics of Ireland. And I'm the guy who just sent it over." He drew himself a Guinness from the tap, then strolled down to the last stool on the end of the bar and gave her a little wave.

Meggie waved back as she took a sip of the rum punch. It was sweet and potent and the perfect fortification for this wicked little game he was intent on playing. She drew a deep breath and steadied her resolve. If she really wanted to begin living a more exciting life, she could start here. "Now what do I do?" she asked, her inhibitions fading with the second sip of the rum punch.

"Well, if you like the drink and you want to get to know me, then I'd suggest you wander over to the jukebox and drop a few quarters in."

"Why?" Meggie asked, looking at him over the rim of her glass.

"Because that will give me a chance to see what a beautiful body you have. And it'll give me a chance to see how you move."

"What if I don't have a beautiful body?" she asked, reality intruding into the little fantasy he'd created.

Dylan groaned, then slid off his stool and strode over to the cash register. He pulled out a handful of quarters, then dropped them on the bar in front of her, leaning over the bar as he spoke. "Sweetheart, if you walked over to the jukebox in a crowded bar, I wouldn't be the only one watching. Now go play some music and quit asking questions."

Meggie grabbed her drink, then walked across to the jukebox. She felt Dylan's eyes on her and she slowed her pace and let her hips sway just a little more than normal. Though she wore a heavy wool sweater and faded jeans, right now she felt positively sexy—and a little bit naughty. She found a Clannad CD and punched in the numbers, then waited for the music to start, her racing heart providing the percussion until it did.

"Hi there."

His breath was warm against her ear and Meggie jumped, surprised that he'd snuck up on her. She spun around. But as she did, she forgot she was still clutching her rum punch. The glass hit his chest and the contents sloshed over the side and soaked the front of his sweater. She cursed softly, then risked a glance up at him. "I'm sorry. I—I didn't realize you were standing so close."

"No problem," he said. He grabbed the hem of his sweater and yanked it up over his head, then tossed it on a nearby table. But the punch had soaked through.

This was what happened when she decided to let loose! With any other man, she might have been able to play the game. But Dylan had a way of rattling her composure and setting her nerves on edge. Just the thought of him touching her...or kissing her...Meggie swallowed convulsively, knowing she was ill-prepared to continue. But desire overwhelmed common sense.

With a hesitant hand, she reached out and touched the wet, sticky spot on his T-shirt. Then she drew a shaky breath and said something that shocked even her. "Maybe you should take your T-shirt off, too," she suggested. "I mean, so I can rinse out the punch."

Dylan eyed her for a long moment, then reached down to tug it off. But she stopped him, emboldened by an uncharacteristic surge of courage. Gathering the soft fabric between her fingers, she slowly pushed it up along his torso, then pulled it over his head. "There," she murmured, her gaze falling on his smooth, muscular chest. "That's better."

He slipped his arm around her waist and pulled her closer, all thoughts of laundry fleeing her head. Meggie pressed her palms against his naked skin, the dusting of hair on his chest soft beneath her fingers. "Now what do we do?" she murmured.

He bent closer, his lips nearly touching her cheek, then whispered in her ear. "I'd ask you if you wanted to play a game of pool or darts."

"Why is that?"

"Because you probably wouldn't know how to play," he explained. "So I would show you and that would give me a chance to touch you."

Meggie rested her head on his shoulder, turning her face up until their lips were just inches apart. "I'd love to play darts or pool," she murmured. The rest of the invitation was silent, yet understood.

She wanted him to touch her—whenever and wherever he wanted to.

"NOW YOU LINE the ball up with the pocket. Find the spot on the ball where you need to hit it with the cue ball and then just...gently...stroke the stick."

"All right," Meggie murmured. She leaned over the pool table, her backside brushing his lap. He groaned inwardly, then wrapped his arms around her as he showed her how to hold the cue. He'd already showed her how to throw darts and just when he thought he couldn't bear it anymore, when he couldn't keep his desire under control, he'd suggested they try a game of pool. But pool hadn't been any easier on the libido than darts.

Dylan wasn't sure how much longer he could play out this little fantasy they'd begun. What started as a silly game had resulted in a very obvious physical reaction—a reaction that was getting harder to ignore by the second.

Had she been any other woman, Dylan might have thrown caution to the wind and seduced her. But this was Meggie. And Meggie was different. He wasn't sure why, but in his mind he held her apart from all the other conquests in his life. Maybe it began as a need to protect her—or at least protect the memory of the vulnerable, introverted girl she'd been. But that had changed long ago, around the time he realized that nothing he did could stop him from wanting her.

He needed her like he'd never needed a woman before. But Dylan suspected that when they did make love, there would be more to it than just a physical release. To say he wasn't a little bit scared would be lie. Meggie was the only woman he'd ever known who had the capacity to touch his heart—and she could break it just as easily.

"It went in!" Meggie cried. She spun around, but Dylan was still bent over with his hands braced on either side of her.

She caught his nose with the cue stick and for a moment he saw stars. He slowly straightened, blinking to clear his head.

"Oh," she cried. "Oh, I'm sorry. I didn't realize you were so...I mean, when I turned, the cue stick just..." She reached up and gently touched his nose. "Does it hurt?"

"I suppose I should be happy I managed to escape darts without serious injury."

"I've never been very good at sports," Meggie admitted. "I get nervous and then I get clumsy." She pushed up on her toes and kissed his nose. "Is that better?"

He smiled grudgingly. "A little better."

Meggie stared at him for a long moment, her expression turning serious. Then she kissed him again, slowly, deliberately, this time on his right cheek. "How about now?" she murmured, her voice low and throaty.

"One more would probably make it feel just fine."

She leaned forward to kiss his other cheek but at the last second, he turned and her lips met his. This time, Dylan didn't take the lead. He let the kiss spin out at Meggie's pace, at first slow and hesitant. But then, she ran her tongue along the crease of his mouth, teasing, tempting him to deepen the kiss. When it came to Meggie, he couldn't resist.

Dylan spanned her waist with his hands and lifted her up to sit on the edge of the pool table, their mouths still caught in a delicate exploration. Then he stepped between her legs and pulled her nearer, molding her body against his naked chest, pulling her thighs around his hips. She was so warm and soft and touchable and no matter where he put his hands, he couldn't get enough of her.

He wanted to stop, but the urge to continue was so much greater. His need for Meggie had become almost a constant in his life. And each time he touched her or kissed her, Dylan knew there would come a time when he couldn't stop himself. His effort at control was weakening and the feel of her palms smoothing over his chest wasn't helping.

Gazing down at her hands, he watched her trace patterns with her fingers, leaving a warm brand on his skin wherever she touched. He wanted her to possess him, to treat his body as if it belonged to her. To take pleasure in making him ache for the sensations of her hands on his skin.

He reached down and tangled his fingers in hers, then drew her hand to his mouth. In the past, seduction had been a game, a means to an end, the ultimate release. But with Meggie, it was just the beginning, like a door opening into her soul. He wanted to know her, both physically and emotionally. He needed to learn what made her happy and sad, what made her shudder with desire and cry out with need.

Dylan started with the soft skin beneath her ear. He pressed his lips to the spot, then gently sucked and nipped. Meggie drew in a sharp breath and he knew he'd had the right effect. Her shoulder was next and Dylan slipped his hand beneath her sweater and tugged it until he found another spot. Slowly, he tested her reaction and before long, she moaned softly, her head tipped back, her eyes closed.

But the heavy wool sweater was becoming a hindrance. Impatient to continue, Dylan reached down and grabbed the hem, then slowly tugged it up. Meggie met his gaze and the desire burning there startled him. She'd been caught by it, too, and it was just as undeniable. With an impatient sigh, she brushed his hands away and in one quick motion, pulled both her sweater and T-shirt off at once. Then she tossed them both aside and shook her head, her hair tumbling around her face and shoulders.

Dylan could barely breathe. She was the most beautiful thing he'd ever seen. Her skin, even under the unflattering lights of the poolroom, was so luminous, so flawless that instinct drove him to spread his hands over her bare shoulders. He pushed one bra strap aside and then the other.

Meggie's teeth chattered and he caught her gaze with his. "Are you cold?" he murmured, rubbing her arms.

She shook her head. Dylan could see a flicker of indecision in her eyes and he was about to call an end to this intimate game. But then she reached out and slipped her fingers beneath the waistband of his jeans. Scooting back onto the pool table she pulled him with her, until he was nearly lying on top of her.

"I'm not very good at this," she murmured.

"Just touch me," Dylan said, dropping a kiss into the curve of her neck. "And I'll touch you. The rest will take care of itself."

Though she'd had experience with men, Dylan suspected she'd never really been well seduced, the kind of seduction where the mind loses touch with the body, where raw instinct takes over and inhibition disappears. He knew he could take her there. It would just take time. Meggie began at the notch in his collarbone, tracing a line with her fingers, then following with her mouth.

When her tongue reached his nipple, he sucked in a sharp breath and moaned softly. She froze, then looked up. "Did I hurt you?"

Dylan smiled, raking his fingers through her hair. "No. That felt incredible."

The notion that she had the power to make him moan seemed to please her and when she went back to kissing his chest, it was with a new purpose. Her hair created a curtain around her face and tickled his belly as she moved lower and lower. And then, she reached out and touched him through the faded fabric of his jeans and Dylan thought he'd go out of his mind.

Nothing had prepared him for this reaction, for the instant need to discard every last bit of clothing, to pull her naked body against his and bury himself deep inside of her. He reached down and grabbed her wrist, then drew her back up until her eyes met his. "Is this what you want?" he murmured.

Meggie nodded.

"Say it," Dylan demanded.

She took a ragged breath. "I do," Meggie said, in voice as clear and determined as he'd ever heard. "I want you." She hesitated, and Dylan was sure she was about to change her mind. "I mean, if you want me, I want you."

He chuckled softly. "Oh, I want you, Meggie. I don't think you realize how much." Dylan grabbed her around the waist and rolled her over until he was on top. He braced his hands on either side of her head and dropped a kiss on her mouth.

"Tell me what you like," Meggie said.

"Just take it slow," Dylan said, dropping another kiss onto her shoulder. "That's what I like."

"Slow," she murmured, as she ran her hand down his chest and dipped her fingers beneath the waistband of his jeans.

"Slow," he repeated, skimming his knuckles over the soft flesh of her breast until they caught the lacy edge of her bra.

And so began a new game designed to rid themselves of their clothes. There were no rules, so they made them up as they went along. Meggie unbuttoned his jeans and he unclasped her bra. She dispensed with the zipper and he tossed aside the scrap of satin and lace.

Her body was so beautiful, so perfect, and with every inch of skin revealed, he found himself needing more. Clothes became a barrier, unneeded and unwanted, and any hint of reticence dissolved beneath his hands and his mouth. He slid her jeans over her hips, then twisted out of his own and pulled her back into his arms.

The feel of her against his body electrified every nerve. Sensations became intensified until the mere thought of her beneath him was enough to push him toward the edge. Dylan tried to control his thoughts, fearful that he'd be done before they'd even started. He'd once considered himself accomplished in the art of seduction, but with Meggie, it was a whole new experience. He felt untried and unschooled, existing from one sensation to the next.

And Meggie wasn't making control easy. Whoever had told her she wasn't good at sex had been sadly mistaken. She combined an insatiable desire with a streak of sweet vulnerability, the contrast so intriguing that he seemed caught in her spell. Yet every now and then, reality hit him full force, in his potent reaction when she wrapped her fingers around him, in the unbidden groan that slipped from his lips and the flood of heat that coursed through his bloodstream.

Their surroundings faded into a blur. They weren't making love on the pool table of Quinn's pub. Nothing existed beyond two naked bodies taking pleasure in each other. And when he could stand it no longer, he drew her up to straddle his hips. Slowly, Dylan ran his hands over her breasts, taking the time to touch every curve, every sweet inch of flesh.

But Meggie wouldn't have any off it. Her skin was flushed and her breath came in short gasps. Dylan reached for his jeans and found the foil packet in his wallet. He tore it open with his teeth and Meggie took the condom from him. Her hands trembled as she sheathed him.

And then she was above him, pausing, waiting. Dylan thought she might stop right there, but then, as he entered her, he realized that she merely wanted to slow their pace, to savor the exquisite feel of their bodies joined in such an intimate way. For a long moment, he was afraid to move, but then he couldn't help himself.

He began slowly, but that plan was quickly forgotten the

minute he got a taste of the delicious heat that raced through his body. Every thought centered on the point where they were joined, every nerve alive. He quickened his pace and Meggie matched him stroke for stroke, her gaze fixed on his.

Dylan saw the changes in her, the arch of her neck, the quickened breathing, the passion-glazed eyes, as their rhythm increased. And when he felt she was near, he touched her. An instant later, she tensed and tightened around him. Her eyes went wide, as if the orgasm was taking her by surprise. And then she shattered, crying out his name.

The sound of her voice snapped the last thread of his control and he tightened his grip on her waist and drove into her one last time. And then, pleasure, more intense and exquisite than he'd ever felt washed over him like a wave, so fierce that he felt as if he were drowning in it.

She collapsed on top of him, naked, sated, her body covered with a sheen of perspiration. Dylan curled his arm around her neck and idly ran his fingers through her hair. Then he rolled her over to lie beside him, nuzzling the soft spot of skin beneath her ear. "I don't ever want to move from this spot," he murmured.

Meggie gave him a drowsy smile. "It's going to be a little hard to put the nine ball in the corner pocket with us lying here. There'll probably be a lot of complaints from the customers."

"They can play around us," he said.

"All right." She sighed softly and wrapped her arm around his waist. And within a few minutes, she was asleep. Dylan closed his eyes. He knew he ought to wake her and take her home. Or at least find something to cover them to keep them warm. But he wanted to let the moment sink in.

He'd made love to Meggie and he knew, without a doubt in his mind, that he'd never make love to another woman in his life. There would be no reason. From now on, there was only Meggie.

MEGGIE SLOWLY OPENED her eyes. An odd blur of lights and shadows teased at her gaze. She squinted, then wondered when she'd installed neon lights in her bedroom. A moment later, she realized she wasn't in her nice soft bed. No, she was lying naked on the pool table in the middle of Quinn's Pub, curled up beneath Dylan's flannel-lined jacket.

She moved slightly, then felt Dylan stir behind her. His arms were wrapped around her, one beneath her head and the other at her waist, and his legs were tangled with hers. He hadn't bothered with clothes, instead keeping warm by tucking his body against hers.

Meggie wasn't sure what to do. She slowly moved her arm until she could see her watch. "Oh, God," she murmured. "That can't be right. Eight fifty-five?" She rolled over then poked Dylan in the shoulder. "Wake up," she pleaded. "Dylan, it's morning and we fell asleep on the pool table."

He groaned softly, then nuzzled his face into the curve of her neck. "What time is it?"

"Almost nine," she said.

"Then go back to sleep. Quinn's doesn't open until eleven."

Meggie sat up, holding the jacket around her as if it might be some antidote for the embarrassment she felt. "I don't intend to be here when your father and brothers arrive. And I was supposed to meet Lana at the shop at eight. She's going to wonder where I am."

She'd always imagined the morning after such a passion-filled night would be just as passionate—waking up to his touch, making love while still half asleep. But then, she'd never expected the most passionate night of her life would occur on a pool table in an Irish pub! "We have to go. I have to go."

Dylan reluctantly sat up then scrubbed the sleep from his eyes with his fists. He raked his hands through his hair and turned to her. "You look beautiful," he said with a drowsy smile.

"Don't you try that smile on me, Dr. Charm. Now get dressed. We have to leave." Meggie wriggled to the edge of the table, then swung her leg over the side. But Dylan caught her before she could jump to the floor.

"I've never been a very good pool player," he teased, "but I have to say, I'm learning to enjoy the game."

"I can't believe I did this," Meggie murmured. "I've never done anything like this in my life." She must have been overly tired. Or maybe it had been the rum punch. But though she should have been mortified by her behavior, Meggie almost felt proud of herself. She'd made a decision to start living for the moment and this certainly was a moment she'd never forget. In truth, she and Dylan had had a couple hundred moments that would be worth reliving over and over again.

She grabbed her clothes from where they'd been tossed on the floor and began to yank them on. But Dylan was still lying on the pool table, watching her, a satisfied smile curling the corners of his mouth. She brushed aside the urge to crawl back on the table and make love to him again, to follow those instincts that had led them to this point. Instead, she crawled underneath the pool table to retrieve her socks and shoes.

When she stood up again, he was still smiling. "Stop it," she said.

"Stop what?"

"Stop looking like the cat who just slept with the canary."

"I'm happy," Dylan said. "So sue me."

He rolled over on his stomach and braced himself with his elbows. He was stark naked, yet he seemed completely at ease with his body. And it was an incredible body, Meggie mused. Like it had been carved by a master sculptor, every muscle and angle filled with pure masculinity.

"You know, I've never done anything like this either," Dylan said.

"Don't lie to me," Meggie said.

His expression turned serious. "Meggie, I'd never lie to you, I swear. And last night was a first, in a lot of ways."

Meggie stared at him for a long moment, gauging the truth in his eyes, afraid to ask him just what he meant. Was this the first time he'd slept with such an inexperienced woman? Or maybe the first time he'd ever seduced a woman so quickly?

She wanted to believe that last night had been just as exciting for him as it had been for her. But common sense overtook wishful thinking.

She tossed aside his jacket and tugged her sweater and T-shirt over her head. "We really should go," she murmured from beneath the twisted sweater. When she finally poked her head through, she searched the floor for her missing sock and found it in the corner pocket, along with her bra. "I'm just going to go to the bathroom and splash some water on my face."

But he caught her arm as she passed and pulled her to him. With the gentlest touch, he cupped her face in his hands and looked deeply into her eyes. "I don't regret a single moment of last night," he murmured, his gaze open and intense. "And I don't want you to either."

Meggie nodded, then hurried off to the bathroom, the last of her clothes clutched in her hands. She flipped on the light and stepped inside, then leaned back against the door. Maybe he hadn't lied to her, but that didn't stop her from feeling like she'd been deceiving him. This whole plan to catch him then dump him had become a weight around her neck. She wasn't sure of her motives anymore.

Did she really expect this to be a one-night stand, an experiment in pleasure meant to end once the sun came up? "I am so dumb," Meggie muttered. Now that it was all over, all she could think about was when it was going to happen again. And again and again.

"Idiot," she said. She quickly tugged on her jeans, then

shoved her underwear into her back pocket. She could finish dressing in the office at the shop. With a wet finger, she did a passable job of brushing her teeth. She'd left her purse in the car, so there was no way to brush her hair.

When she emerged from the bathroom, Dylan was only half dressed. His jeans were unbuttoned and he was shirtless. He braced a hip against the pool table, then smiled.

"What?" she murmured.

"Meggie, I meant what I said. Last night was special. I know you probably don't believe that. I guess I wouldn't either, considering my record with women, but I just wanted you to know that—"

Meggie stepped forward and threw her arms around his neck. Her kiss put an end to his explanations and to her nagging need to take just a little bit of last night with her to work. "We have to go. Now."

She handed him his T-shirt and his sweater, still stained with a red splotch from the rum punch. Then she dragged him toward the door. But before he opened it, Dylan caught her up in his arms and kissed her once more, long and hard, as if reminding her of exactly what had happened the night before.

But Meggie didn't need any reminders. As they walked to the car, she recalled the way he responded to her touch. And as they pulled away from the curb, she remembered the sensation of his hips nestled between her thighs. There'd been that moment, when she'd straddled his hips and he slowly entered her—that one heart-stopping instant, that very first sensation, when they became one. No matter what happened between them, she'd always have that memory. It would never fade.

Dylan wove expertly through traffic. Every now and then, Meggie would risk a glance over at him. He seemed so happy, satisfied, a smile curving the corners of his mouth. They didn't talk much in the car and Meggie suspected that he was as occupied with thoughts of their night together as she was. Though she tried to focus on the day ahead, on all things she had to do at the shop, tantalizing images kept creeping back into her mind—naked skin, tangled limbs and the sheer pleasure of touching a perfect male body.

The next time she looked out at the street, they were parked in front of the shop. Suddenly, Meggie wished they'd stayed at the pub just a little longer.

Dylan draped his arm over the back of her seat. "Can I see you tonight?" he murmured.

"I have to go to a party. For my grandmother. It's her eightieth birthday."

"I could take you," he murmured as he toyed with her hair.

His offer surprised her. First an afternoon with his brothers, then mad, passionate love on the pool table of his father's pub. And now, a Flanagan family gathering? "Are you offering because you want to see me or do you want to spend time with my family?"

"Both," Dylan said. "I haven't seen your parents for ages. And I'd like to see Tommy again. But mostly, I'm not sure I can go twenty-four hours without seeing you."

"All right," she said.

He wove his fingers through the hair at her nape then gently pulled her closer. His kiss was incredibly sweet and gentle and given the choice, Meggie would have spent the whole day in his car doing nothing but kissing him. But Lana was waiting. When Dylan finally drew back, she gave him a shaky smile. "I better go. I'll see you tonight."

Meggie hopped out of the car and ran toward the shop. She felt like skipping and shouting and spinning around until she was dizzy. She'd just spent the most incredible night of her life. But as she spied Lana through the window of the shop, reality began to set it. Nothing this perfect ever lasted. Sooner or later Dylan would move on to someone else and she'd be left with only memories. Olivia's words came back to her, risks versus rewards. "I knew the risks," she murmured as she yanked open the door. "And I enjoyed the rewards. I have no right to complain about the consequences."

Lana was sitting at the counter when Meggie walked in, perched on a stool, the morning paper spread out in front of her. She glanced up, observing her shrewdly. "You're late," she said.

"I decided to sleep in. After the grand opening, we're both going to have early mornings and late nights. I thought I'd take advantage of the time while I still had it."

"How was your date?"

Meggie gave her a nonchalant shrug. "It was fine. We helped take his brother Brendan's boat up to Gloucester. His older brother, Conor, and his fiancée, Olivia came with. It was a beautiful day."

"You spent the day with his brothers?" Lana asked.

Meggie nodded.

A slow smile broke across her face. "This is it," she said, her voice filled with excitement. "It's actually working. And so much faster then I thought it would."

"What are you talking about?"

"A guy like Dylan Quinn doesn't introduce just any old girlfriend to his brothers. This is a big moment and you didn't even realize it."

Though Meggie wanted to believe her words, she'd learned to be cautious with Lana's proclamations. "Olivia did say that I was the first girl he'd ever brought along on *The Mighty Quinn*."

"That's good, that's very good. And what about your third date? Did you make plans?"

Meggie knew she was about to get a scolding for breaking the rules. But she didn't care. After all the rules she broke last night, there wasn't much point. "We're going out tonight. I know, I broke the four-day rule, but I have to go to my grandmother's birthday party and I thought it might be nice to take a date along. My mother is always wondering why I don't have a social life. Maybe this will satisfy her for the next few years."

"I'm surprised he agreed to go."

"He offered," Meggie said.

Lana hopped off her stool and circled the counter, then

pulled out the most recent revision of her flowchart. She smoothed it out and stared at it for a long time. "I think I might have to make another revision. This guy is moving really fast. That must be because you've been playing hard to get." She smiled. "A guy like him only does the family thing if he's falling in love."

Meggie's heart stopped as Lana said the words. Love? Could she really believe that Dylan was falling in love with her after only two dates? She held her breath and waited for her heart to start again. When it did, she gulped back a surge of panic. "That can't be right. He couldn't be falling in love with me. It's too soon." Besides, even she knew that sex didn't always mean love to a man, especially a man like Dylan Quinn.

"Why not? You've been following the plan, haven't you?"

"Yes," Meggie lied. Lana's plan had barely even entered her mind during the past twenty-four hours. The only thing she'd been following was her instincts...her hormones...her overwhelming desires.

"I think it's time to put him to the test."

"I'm not sure I like the sound of that."

"It's simple. We introduce another element to the flow-chart. We'll call him...David."

"I don't know any David," Meggie said.

Lana gave her a sly smile. "Neither do I. But Dylan Quinn won't know that."

Meggie sat down onto a stool and watched as Lana began to scribble on a scrap of paper. But she couldn't think about the plan. The plan wasn't working. It wasn't in the plan for her to enjoy his touch and crave his kisses. It wasn't in the plan to make love to him on their second date or to lie about it all to her best friend.

And it certainly wasn't in the plan for her to fall head-over-heels in love with him for the second time in her life.

6

"I'LL BE READY in a minute," Meggie said, racing from the front door to her bedroom.

Dylan glanced around her apartment. She'd greeted him, flushed and breathless, and still dressed in jeans and the sweater she'd worn last night. On the drive over he'd thought about how it would be seeing her for the first time after what had happened on the pool table at the pub. Would the desire be instant and intense? Would they tumble into her bed within the first few moments together and relive the passion they'd shared the night before?

In the seconds after she opened the door, he'd looked into her eyes for a hint of regret or embarrassment. But she'd turned away so quickly that he hadn't had time to kiss her much less gauge her mood. All he knew was that she wasn't thinking about ripping her clothes off and seducing him.

"Just make yourself at home," she shouted. "There's juice in the fridge. Or wine. I don't think I have beer." She peeked out of the door. "I'm sorry I'm late. I got hung up at the shop and I didn't realize the time. If I'm late for Nonna May's party my mother will kill me."

She slammed the bedroom door and Dylan stood in the middle of the living room, frowning. This was not the way it was supposed to go. There was supposed to be at least an acknowledgement of what had happened, maybe a sexy smile or a provocative comment. Or at least a lingering, tantalizing kiss. He strode across the room and knocked on the door.

Meggie opened it a crack. "What?"

He firmly pushed against the door until it gave way, then stepped into Meggie's bedroom. She was dressed in just her jeans and the lacy scrap of a bra that he'd removed once before. Without giving her time to protest, he wrapped an arm around her waist and pulled her against him, then kissed her long and hard.

His hands skimmed over her body in an unspoken possession, reminding himself of the feel of her, the way her curves fit his touch. Reminding her of what that touch could do to her body. When he finally released her from his embrace, Dylan was satisfied that her desire for him hadn't abated since they'd last been together. If anything it had grown more acute.

He stared down at her face. Her eyes were still closed and her lips were damp and slightly swollen. She waited for him to take her again, a tiny, but satisfied smile on her lips. But Dylan wanted to leave her aching for more. "There," he said. "Now that we've taken care of the important stuff, you can get dressed."

She opened her eyes, then gasped softly as he walked back to the door and closed it behind him. A low chuckle rumbled in his chest. He'd thought he'd experienced it all. He was thirty-one years old, a grown man by almost every standard—except maybe his own—a man with his share of experience with women. Yet a few seconds with Meggie was all it took to make him realize he hadn't experienced anything yet.

Until he met Meggie, his life had been set. He had his job, a nice place to live, brothers who cared about him and women who didn't care too much. Life had been good and he hadn't imagined it could get any better. But then Meggie had come along and she turned everything upside down. Suddenly, he found himself wanting much more from every hour of every day. It wasn't enough just to live. There was something he was searching for, something vague and elusive, something he could only find with Meggie in his arms.

But even though he'd spent a fair amount of time with her, he still felt she was holding back, keeping her emotions in check. She didn't completely trust him and he hadn't been able to change that. It was as if she, like his brothers, expected him to screw up, expected him to revert to the old Dylan Quinn behavior. Maybe he just needed a little more time to prove himself.

Dylan wandered around the living room, idly picking up photos and knickknacks, trying to get handle on the woman he'd made love to last night, the woman who could turn from demure to passionate in the blink of an eye. On her desk, he found a picture of Meggie with her family. It was an old picture, taken when she still had braces and wore glasses.

This was the girl he remembered. But as he stared at it closely, Dylan saw beyond first impressions, past the silly haircut and the horn-rimmed glasses and the mouthful of metal. Why hadn't he noticed before? She'd been beautiful even back then. She just hadn't grown into her features. Her sensual mouth and high cheekbones, her wide eyes, looked odd on a girl her age. But they were perfect on a woman.

Dylan smiled. Maybe it was lucky it had taken her awhile to attain her true beauty. Had anyone noticed her in high school, she might already have been happily married with three kids, a dog and a house in the suburbs. And by the time he'd pulled her out of her shop, it would have been too late.

He'd never been one to believe in fate or karma. Everything happened for a reason. But maybe it was fate that had put that defective espresso machine in her shop. And it could have been fate that made the machine go haywire during his shift. Whatever it was, he'd met Meggie at the right time and for that he considered himself lucky.

After all, she could have easily had a boyfriend or a fiancé and then where would he... Dylan stopped short just as he was about to continue his tour with a stroll around her kitchen. Tucked away on the counter next to the stove he noticed a huge bouquet of flowers, long-stemmed roses. The kind that cost a week's salary for a couple dozen. He took a quick look over his shoulder, then snatched the card from amongst the elegant flowers.

Suddenly, his little bouquet of roses didn't seem nearly impressive enough. This bouquet stood almost three feet tall. And whoever had sent it, had meant to make a statement. He pulled the card from the envelope. *"Until I see you again,"* he murmured. *"David."*

Dylan scowled as he carefully placed the card back into the flowers. "Who the hell is David?" he muttered. And more importantly, what was he doing sending Meggie—his Meggie—flowers? Dylan made a mental note of the florist's name. Maybe Conor could use his influence to find out a little more about... He groaned softly, then turned away from the counter. Was he crazy? How could he expect Meggie to trust him if he didn't trust her?

If she did have another man in hot pursuit, then he had only one option. He'd do his best to convince Meggie that he was the only man in her life. "Nice flowers," he shouted as he walked back into the living room.

Meggie peeked out the bedroom door again, her hair twisted into a towel. "They are nice," she said before closing the door again.

"Yeah, right," Dylan muttered. "Real nice." He walked over to the sofa and sat down, his mind spinning with all the possibilities. David couldn't be a real serious threat. After all, Meggie had made love to *him* last night, and she wasn't the type to take something like that lightly.

Dylan leaned back into the cushions, then heard a crunch beneath him. He reached around and grabbed a crumbled wad of paper from behind a pillow. Smoothing the sheet over his thigh, Dylan tried to read the printing. It was a flowchart. At first he assumed it had something to do with Meggie's business. But as he looked at it in greater detail he realized it was a very unusual plan. From what he could tell, it was plan to catch a man—and that man was him!

He quickly crumpled it back up and hid it behind the pillow, certain that it was never meant for his eyes. But his curiosity got the better of him and Dylan retrieved it. There was a red circle around one box that said "Send Self Flowers." But it was the box at the top that caused the most confusion, the box with "revenge" in big capital letters.

"So, are you really ready to spend a night with my crazy relatives?" Meggie asked as she walked back into the room.

Dylan shoved the paper into his jacket pocket then rose to his feet. She looked incredible, dressed in a figure-skimming black dress that hugged every curve. The neckline dipped just low enough to reveal an expanse of soft skin. Her hair was swept up, allowing a tempting view of her neck. And the skirt was short enough to show off her beautiful legs. He instantly forgot the paper stuffed in his pocket and wrapped an arm around her waist. "We could always stay here and call in our birthday greetings," he said. "They'd never notice we weren't there."

Her smile faded slightly. "If you'd rather not go along, I can understand. Doing the family thing probably isn't your—"

He put a finger to her lips. "I was teasing. I want to go. Really."

She nodded, then turned and grabbed her coat from the back of the sofa. "My Aunt Doris will probably be at the party," Meggie said as she walked to the door. "Avoid her at all costs. If you don't, you'll get a recap of her recent gall bladder surgery and the resulting gastrointestinal problems. And

Uncle Roscoe is a compulsive gambler, so if he tries to talk you into a bet, make sure it's only for a few dollars. And my cousin Randy, has a—"

"Meggie."

"—really obnoxious habit of eating off of—"

"Meggie!"

She turned and looked at him, her eyes wide. "What?"

"I'll be fine. I think I can hold my own with your family. It's not like I've never met them."

"Of course you can. I didn't mean to imply—"

"Of course, you didn't," he teased.

"It's just that they'll probably think that you're my boyfriend and—"

This time, Dylan didn't bother to interrupt. He grabbed her arm and pulled her back into his arms, then stared down into her eyes. "All right. I think we need to get something straight here." His jaw went tight and his temper was just barely in check. "Have you forgotten what happened last night? Or did I imagine the whole thing?"

A blush crept up her cheeks and she fixed her gaze on his chest. "No," she said in a tiny voice.

"If any of your relatives want to think I'm your boyfriend or your sweetheart or even your lover, I'm not going to object. Because as far as I'm concerned I'm all three. Got that?"

She blinked, then opened her mouth to speak. But Meggie seemed so taken aback by his statement that she wasn't sure what to say. Rather than wait for a comment, he hooked his finger under her chin and closed her mouth, then brushed a quick kiss across her lips. "Good. Then it's settled," he said. "And by the way, you can throw those flowers away. If David has any questions about why you don't want to see him anymore, you can just tell him to call me."

MEGGIE STARED OUT the windshield of Dylan's Mustang, watching the familiar sights go by as they drove to her parents' house in South Boston. She glanced over at Dylan, only to find his attention focused on the street. With a soft sigh, Meggie leaned back into the seat. Though Dylan had already met her parents and her brother, she still couldn't help but be a little nervous.

She'd never brought a man to any family function. And considering her parents' desire to see her happily married and raising their grandchildren, she knew they'd jump to conclusions. Knowing her mother, she'd be ready to start the wedding plans. But Meggie intended to remind Maura Flanagan of the pain Dylan Quinn had caused her all those years ago.

Her mother had been there that night after the Frolic when she'd cried herself to sleep. Even now, Meggie could remember her mother's words—how someday she'd look back on the night and laugh about it. How it was all part of growing up. And how love wasn't always a smooth ride. Meggie groaned inwardly. If only she had been able to laugh about it. Then maybe she wouldn't be caught in the middle of this mess.

She really should jump out of the car and find a pay phone.

Lana would be so happy to hear that the flowers she'd sent to Meggie's apartment did exactly what they were supposed to do, even though Meggie had done her best to hide them. Dylan was now officially her boyfriend, a big leap up the flowchart to the ultimate goal. But though Meggie should have been happy, all she could muster was a severe case of guilt.

This plan had gotten completely out of control! She'd manipulated him and he'd fallen for it. She'd never expected the plan to work and now that it had, she wasn't quite sure what to do. He'd fallen for her under false pretenses and though she hadn't really broken any laws, she still felt regret. How could she ever know if his feelings were true or just a result of her manipulation?

Dylan pulled the car over to the curb in front of her house and turned off the ignition. "We're here," Meggie murmured, staring out at the little frame house painted a cheery shade of yellow.

"Don't worry," he said. "If I do anything wrong, you just tug on your ear and we'll head straight to the door." With that, he twisted around and grabbed something out of the back seat—an elaborately wrapped gift with a beautiful fabric bow and expensive wrapping paper.

"What's that?" she asked.

"It's a present for your grandmother," he said. "You told me it was her birthday, right?"

"Oh," Meggie murmured. "Right. That was nice of you. Very thoughtful."

Dylan toyed with the bow. "Olivia helped me pick it out.

It's an antique silver picture frame from the Victorian era. I don't really know what that means but it's really pretty. Olivia assured me that your grandmother would like it and Olivia knows things like that."

Meggie glanced down at the gift on her lap. How was it that a complete stranger knew the perfect gift to get her Nonna May and all she'd managed was a package of embroidered handkerchiefs? Maybe it was because Dylan Quinn had charm down to a science. "She'll love it."

She stared out the window as Dylan hopped out of the car, suddenly filled with regret over inviting him. She wanted to believe that he really cared, that he wasn't just turning on the charisma for her grandmother's sake. But if he really cared, then she'd have to face the fact that she cared, too. More than she'd ever intended to.

Dylan reached out to help her from the car and as they walked up to the house, he held her hand. But a moment before her mother answered the doorbell, Meggie tugged her hand from his and fiddled with the bow on her present.

The door swung open. "Meggie!" Maura Flanagan gathered her daughter into a welcoming hug, crushing the present between them. "It seems like ages since we've seen you." Then she glanced at Meggie's "date" and raised an eyebrow. "Who is this? I think I know this boy."

"It's Dylan, Mom. Dylan Quinn. Tommy's old friend."

"Dylan Quinn?" Without a second thought, Meggie's mother grabbed him and gave him a hug as fierce as Meggie's had been. "My, look how you've grown! Such a handsome man. What are you doing here? Did Tommy invite you?"

"When Meggie told me about the party, I just had to come. I was hoping I'd get some of that wonderful cooking of yours. I wasn't wrong, was I?"

Maura looped her arm through Dylan's and walked with him into the house, leaving Meggie alone on the porch to stare after them. The man could charm the white off rice. Her mother knew exactly the pain he'd caused her. She'd been the one to reassure Meggie that all her friends in high school would never remember that Dylan was supposed to take her to the dance.

"Traitor," she muttered as she stepped inside. "Dr. Charm strikes again."

By the time she got her coat off, Dylan had already joined the party. He'd been greeted warmly by her brother Tommy and her father. Then he moved on to Nonna May, squatting down beside her chair to offer birthday greetings. Meggie watched him from across the room, watched the easy way he interacted with her family. It was as if he belonged here and she was the outsider.

For a moment, she almost wished he was her boyfriend. She'd never had a man in her life who she felt was important enough to introduce to her family. But everyone loved Dylan. He was funny and handsome and completely at ease. And who could resist that smile? When he turned it on, anyone would feel like the most special person in the world.

"I didn't know you were dating Dylan Quinn."

Meggie glanced over her shoulder to find her mother standing behind her. "We're not dating," she murmured. "We're just friends." And lovers, she added silently. "He's a firefighter and he put out that fire at the shop. That's how we met again."

"Just friends? If you're just friends, why did you ask him to Nonna May's party?"

"I didn't really ask. He offered to bring me," Meggie said.

Maura's eyes went wide. "He offered?" A slow smile brightened her dubious expression. "He must really like you, Mary Margaret. And it's obvious from that look on your face that the feelings are mutual." Maura nodded knowingly. "He's a good man, he has a good job. You could do much worse."

"Have you forgotten what he did to me in high school?" Meggie asked, lowering her voice and leaning closer to her mother. "How he dumped me and sent his little brother to take me to the Sophomore Frolic. I was completely humiliated. I cried for two days."

Maura scoffed, then waved her hand. "Such old news. You were both kids." She gave Meggie's elbow a squeeze. "I have to fill the punch bowl. Tell your brother he needs to get ice from the fridge in the basement."

Meggie wandered through the living room to the dining room where Tommy was chatting with Dylan. When she stepped up to them, Dylan casually slipped his arm around her waist and smiled at her. Tommy gave her a sly look then grinned. "Well, little sister, you're just full of surprises. I didn't expect you to show up, much less bring along my old buddy, Dylan."

"This is a nice party," Dylan said, his gaze still fixed on her. "I'm glad you invited me."

Meggie forced a smile. "Can I borrow my brother for a while? We need to get some ice." Dylan nodded and Meggie grabbed Tommy's arm and dragged him to the kitchen. When they were out of earshot of Dylan, she scowled up at him. "How could you be so nice to him?"

"What are you talking about? That's Dylan. He's an old friend. And it looks like you two are getting pretty cozy. I never would have thought that—"

"Of course you wouldn't have!" she snapped. "That's because you know exactly what he did to me in high school!"

"What?"

"The Sophomore Frolic?" Meggie reminded him. "He was supposed to take me and at the last minute he sent his brother instead. I told all my friends I had a date with Dylan Quinn and then he stood me up. I was completely humiliated."

"Dylan was never supposed to take you," Tommy said, giving her a look that said she'd just lost her mind. "Why would he take you? You were a sophomore and he was senior, never mind that you were a geek. Let's face it, Megs, guys like Dylan didn't date girls like you."

"But you told me he wanted to take me," Meggie insisted.

"No, I didn't. You were going on and on about that stupid dance, so I asked Dylan if he'd set up a date for you with one of his brothers. I thought he'd send Brendan, but then he sent one of the twins. What's your complaint? You had a date, didn't you?"

Meggie's eyes went wide and she gasped. "What are you saying?"

"What are *you* saying? Are you mad at him because he didn't take you instead of his little brother?"

"No!" Meggie cried. When he said it like that it sounded so...petty and immature. It wasn't a grudge, just a few hurt feelings and a lot of bad memories and scars that ran deeper than she wanted to admit. "No, I...I just thought he was supposed to take me, that's all." She swallowed hard, unable to think straight. "Mom needs ice. She wants you to get it for her."

Once Tommy had left the kitchen, she glanced around, then hurried toward her bedroom. She needed time to think! Had she been wrong all along about Dylan Quinn? Had she somehow convinced herself that he was the one who was supposed to take her to the dance? Meggie groaned softly, then pressed her fingers to her lips, biting back a quiet curse. But just as she reached for the door to her bedroom, the sound of Dylan's voice stopped her.

"Meggie?"

She spun around and pasted a smile on her face. The urge to apologize to him was the first thing that came to mind. But then, he wasn't aware of how she'd been feeling since the day she and Lana had put their silly plan together—a plan that suddenly didn't have any purpose. "Hi," she murmured. Her face felt hot and she knew she was blushing.

"Is everything all right?"

She tried to keep calm, maintaining a tenuous hold on her composure. How could she have been so wrong? He wasn't at fault, she was! "I'm fine," she said. "I was just going to get something from my purse. It's in my room."

"Show me your room," Dylan said. "I'm curious."

The room was exactly the way she'd left it when she'd graduated from college. It was filled with all the mementos of a girl whose life revolved around her studies. There wasn't a single picture of a boyfriend or a dried-up corsage or a love letter. Her crush on Dylan had been such a secret, she allowed no evidence of it in her surroundings. Meggie opened the door. Sadly, she had nothing to hide.

"So how many boys have you invited into this room?" Dylan teased as he strolled around.

His question brought a soft laugh. "Are you kidding?"

"No," Dylan said.

"You're the first boy—or man—except my father or my brother who has ever set foot in here."

He grabbed her around the waist and pulled her up against his body, kissing the curve of her neck. "I'm like Neil Armstrong on the moon or Christopher Columbus in the New World. I guess I should be honored." He pulled her along to a bulletin board that she'd put up to hold all her memories. "Look at this," he said, pointing to a certificate. "Perfect attendance."

She wasn't going to tell him that the reason she'd never missed a day during her sophomore year was because she couldn't give up a chance to see him at school. She'd even gone to school with the flu and a raging fever just hoping to catch sight of him in the hall, praying that he'd smile or say hello. "I know. It's silly."

"No," he protested. "It's nice. I've always wanted to go with a smart girl."

"Is that what we're doing?" she asked. "Are we going together?"

He turned her around and stared down into her eyes. "I guess I always figured that went along with being boyfriend and girlfriend...and lovers. Was I wrong?"

Meggie drew a ragged breath, fixing her gaze on the front of his shirt. Her fingers toyed with a button and she searched for the words to keep the conversation lighthearted. "That's a pretty serious move for a guy like you," she said.

"I feel pretty serious about you."

She glanced up at him, then sighed. "I don't know whether to believe you or not. For all I know, you're just turning on the charm again. You do have a reputation, you know. And don't think I didn't notice how you completely charmed my mother."

His smile faded and his embrace wasn't quite so close. Meggie held her breath. Had she said something to hurt him? A knock sounded at the door and Dylan turned away to look as Tommy popped his head inside. "Hey, Quinn. Me and the cousins are going to play a game of touch football on the street. We need you to even the teams."

His hands slipped from her waist and he sent her a questioning glance. "Go ahead," she said. "I have to help my mom with the food anyway."

He strode out of the room with Tommy and Meggie let out a long breath. Then she turned and flopped facedown on her bed. A groan slipped from her lips. She was going to have to have a serious discussion with Lana tomorrow morning. There had to be a way to reverse the flow of the flowchart and extricate herself from the mess she'd made of her relationship with Dylan Quinn.

"We'll just make another plan and set another goal," she said, her voice muffled in her pillow. Meggie pushed up on her elbows and considered the notion for a long moment. But formulating a new plan would require telling Lana that she'd been lying since the start of their first plan.

She could always carry on by herself, relying on her own instincts. But those were the very same instincts that told her to make love to Dylan Quinn on a pool table! And those were the instincts that had convinced her that what she and Dylan shared might just be something worth preserving.

"So either you make him love you forever or you break up with him," Meggie said. But somehow, she suspected that either option was much easier said than done.

DYLAN STARED AT the morning paper, reading the same column over and over again. Though he was trying hard to concentrate, he wasn't comprehending a single word. In truth, nothing he did to occupy his thoughts had any effect on what was running through his mind.

He hadn't believed Tommy at first. It began as an offhand comment during the touch football game. But then, when they were sharing a beer on the porch, Tommy had mentioned it again. He'd said he was surprised that Meggie and Dylan were friends, much less involved.

Dylan had assumed the comment was based on his reputation with women. But when Tommy went on to explain the grudge that Meggie still harbored, Dylan pressed for more details. Suddenly, everything made sense—Meggie's early hostility, her sudden change of heart. And especially the big capital letters across the paper he'd found in her apartment. REVENGE. That's what all this had been about! Getting back at him for some imagined slight that happened so long ago he could barely remember.

The rest of the party had passed at a grinding pace and he'd found himself looking for other clues, in her expression, in her behavior, in the way she spoke to him. And when it came time to leave, Dylan drove her home and left her at her front door, so preoccupied with his thoughts that anything else, including a good-night kiss or plans for the next night, had fled from his mind.

Even now Dylan couldn't believe it. Meggie had been under the impression that *he* was supposed to take her to that silly dance her sophomore year. Instead, he'd showed up with his little brother in tow, a favor he'd done for Tommy and for Meggie—or so he'd thought.

He recalled her words that very first day, when he'd pulled her from her smoky coffee shop, about how he'd come to ruin her life all over again. Was that really what he'd done? Dylan raked his hand through his hair and stared down at the newspaper. Why couldn't he make sense of this? He hadn't imagined her reactions that night in the pub. It would have taken an incredibly coldhearted woman to fake something like that. But then, what did he really know about Meggie and her true feelings? She kept everything bottled up inside of her.

He cursed softly, then pushed back his chair. "I need some fresh air," he murmured to the group gathered around the table.

But as he was descending the stairs, he saw a familiar figure coming toward him through the garage doors. He stopped on the stairs and called out. "Hey, Con! What are you doing here?"

"I had to interview a witness downtown and I thought I'd drop by."

Dylan frowned as he descended the rest of the way. "You never just drop by. You always have a reason."

"Well, I'm on an official errand for Olivia," he said with a sheepish grin. "She's planning her first dinner party since we've been engaged and she's all excited about it. I told her we could send out for pizza, but she wants to do it right."

"What does this have to do with me?" Dylan asked.

"I'm here to extend an invitation to you and Meggie."

Dylan drew a long breath, then let it out slowly. This was what he got for bringing Meggie along that day on *The Mighty Quinn*. Now everyone assumed that they were a couple.

"That's really nice, but I'm not sure Meggie and I are going to be able to make it."

"Well, we're flexible on the date," Conor said. "And it's nothing real fancy, so—"

"That's not what I meant," Dylan interrupted. "I'm not sure that Meggie and I are going to make it work."

Conor stared at him for a long time. Dylan could see the disappointment in his eyes, the silent accusation that this was just the same old behavior all over again. "You want to tell me what's going on?"

Dylan reached in his shirt pocket and pulled out the paper he'd found at Meggie's apartment, determined to provide a decent excuse. He sat down on one of the bottom steps and watched as Conor looked it over. Dylan had looked at it so many times that he had it memorized. In all honesty, it was an ingenious plan. It capitalized on every male weakness, employing subtle manipulation and carefully timed retreat, the old "why buy the cow" theory. For a woman who claimed to have little experience with men, Meggie knew precisely what made them tick.

"What is this?" Conor asked, flipping it over to examine the back.

"It's a battle plan. To make me fall in love with Meggie Flanagan so that she can dump me and pay me back for something that happened thirteen years ago. It's all there." He punched at the paper with his finger. "And what's even more amazing is that it worked."

"It worked?"

"Yeah," Dylan muttered. "I think I'm in love with Meggie Flanagan."

Conor chuckled. "You say that the same way a guy might say, 'I think I have a social disease.' Or 'I think I just ran over your cat.' You're not very enthusiastic."

"The minute I admit I love her, she's going to dump me," Dylan said, throwing up his hands. "And if I don't say the words, then we'll just go on playing this game. Sooner or later, she'll get bored or impatient or frustrated and she'll dump me anyway. It's a lose-lose situation."

"A woman dump you? Now there's an original concept. Have you ever been dumped before?"

"That's not the point," Dylan said. "The point is that I don't *want* to be dumped. Not this time." He sighed. "I thought what we had was real. I thought I was done with all the games. And now I find the games never ended."

"So what are you going to do?" Conor asked.

"What can I do?" Dylan countered.

"We could always go get a cup of coffee," Conor teased. "I hear there's a new place just down the street."

"Very funny," Dylan said. "Do you have any other witty comments before I kick your butt around the block?"

"Well, I'll just tell you this, little brother. If you really love Meggie Flanagan, then don't let anything keep you apart. Fix the problem. It's not always supposed to be easy, you know. In fact, sometimes it's downright difficult. But at the end of the day, it's what's in your heart, not your head, that really matters."

"Do you ever have any doubts?" Dylan asked, looking up at his big brother. "I mean, about you and Olivia. Do you ever wonder if maybe she's not the one and you're just fooling yourself?"

"Never," Conor said with unwavering conviction. "Do you have doubts about Meggie?"

"No," Dylan said. "And that's what scares me. Am I just deluding myself here?"

"I don't think so."

"So what do I do? I've never been in this position before."

"Maybe you ought to get a plan of your own. Look at this," he said, waving the paper under Dylan's nose. "She's just waiting for you to admit how you feel. So do it. Tell her you love her. And then pray like hell that somewhere along the line, she fell in love with you."

"But what if she didn't," Dylan asked. "Then that would be the end of it."

"Then do everything in direct opposition of her plan. If you don't admit you love her, you could probably keep seeing her indefinitely. And, hell, Dylan, you're a lovable guy. She can't resist you forever."

Dylan stood up and slapped Conor on the shoulder. "Thanks for stopping by. And for the advice."

"What about the dinner party?" Conor asked.

"Can I wait to give you an answer on that? Just tell Olivia I have to check my calendar."

Dylan watched as his brother walked to the door, then gave him a wave before he stepped outside. He raked his fingers through his hair and tried to put his mind to the task at hand. There had to be a way to make this work with Meggie, to turn her plan back against her and make her see that they belonged together. He reached for the pencil in his pocket, then grabbed the clipboard that they used to write down addresses of fires.

"I'll just make a plan of my own," he murmured, sitting down on a nearby bench. "And I'll make it work."

7

MEGGIE STARED AT the stream of coffee as it dribbled into the carafe, counting the minutes, then the seconds before she'd be able to pour a cup and take a sip. After another sleepless night spent tossing and turning, the only antidote for her exhaustion was a cup of Hawaiian Kona, extra strong, in all its caffeinated glory. When the carafe was half full, she flipped off the coffeemaker and filled her cup, then added a generous dose of cream and sugar.

The first sip was like heaven, the caffeine brushing the cobwebs from her brain. But no matter how much she drank, Meggie knew she wouldn't be able to block out the worries that nagged at her mind.

It was over. She'd seen the clues three nights ago, after her grandmother's birthday party. And though she'd always expected the time would come sooner or later, now that it was here, she couldn't believe it had all happened so fast. Dylan was starting to draw away and it began at Nonna's birthday party.

How many times had she rewound the night in her head, trying to figure out the exact moment when the tide had turned, when, instead of taking a step closer to her, Dylan took a step back? And then another and another, until by the time he said good-night to her at her front door he'd been distant and cool.

She should have never allowed him to accompany her. She knew that attending a family gathering was a big step, too much pressure, too many expectations, especially so early in their relationship. But he'd been the one to press her forward, the one who insisted that she consider him her boyfriend.

All along, she had told herself she was no match for Dylan and now she'd proved it. She'd made a mistake and though she wasn't sure what it had been, she knew it had to be her fault. Meggie took another sip of her coffee, then rubbed her forehead, trying to quell the headache that had begun the moment she got out of bed at dawn that morning.

The bell above the door jingled and Meggie turned to watch Lana walk in. All the lies she'd told her best friend had come back to haunt her and now, when she needed a friend the most, she couldn't bring herself to tell Lana what had happened.

"Morning!" Lana called, her eyes bright and her pale skin rosy from the cold.

"Morning," Meggie replied in a feeble attempt to match her good mood.

Lana stopped short, a few feet away from the counter. A tiny frown wrinkled her brow and she stared at Meggie intently. "What's wrong?"

Meggie felt the tears press at the corners of her eyes but she refused to give into them. Tears would only be proof that Dylan Quinn had broken her heart all over again. The first time, she thought she'd never recover. But in hindsight, that had been nothing, merely a twinge, compared to the ache that tightened like a fist around her heart.

"Did something happen with Dylan?" Lana asked, quietly taking the stool beside Meggie's.

Meggie nodded and drew in a shaky breath. "Yeah, something. Actually, a lot of things. I just wish I knew what they were."

"Do you want to talk about it?" Lana asked.

Meggie shifted uneasily on the stool then turned to her friend. "If I tell you, I don't think you're going to be very happy with me." She drew another breath and pressed on. "But we're best friends and we're business partners and I think you need to keep an open mind and understand how much this has been worrying me."

Lana nodded her head. "You're in love with Dylan Quinn," she said.

Meggie gasped. She'd never said the words out loud, only imagined them. "What?"

"You heard me. You're in love with Dylan Quinn." Lana grabbed Meggie's coffee mug and took a sip, watching her over the rim.

When she put down the coffee, Lana was smiling. Meggie buried her face in her hands. Her cheeks were hot against her palms. "How did you know?" she muttered.

"Because I'm the one who made it happen," Lana proclaimed.

"What?" Meggie asked as her head snapped up.

Lana slipped out of her jacket. "My plan. Don't you see? You never would have gone near him without my plan. And I knew once you went out a few times, you'd fall in love. It was all so simple." Lana wiggled her fingers. "And I was pulling all the strings. So, when did you two finally...you know. And don't lie to me. I would have jumped into bed with him after the first date and I've had great sex in the last decade."

Meggie groaned. "I'm so naive. I can't believe I fell for this. You totally manipulated me! This was all supposed to be about revenge and you made it all about...love." The last word came out on a strangled groan.

"No," Lana protested, "it was supposed to be about restoring the balance in your love live. And I did that. You're in love, aren't you?"

"Yes! But that was never part of the plan. At least not the plan I was operating under."

Lana wrapped her arm around Meggie's shoulders and put on a playful pout. "You forgive me, don't you? Because you can't be mad at me for too long. After all, because of me you probably had the best sex you've ever had in your life. And more importantly, I have to be the maid of honor at your wedding so you can't hate me."

"There isn't going to be a wedding," Meggie said.

"Of course there will be a wedding," Lana insisted. "That's the whole reason I did this. So I can wear a silly bridesmaid's dress and spend the entire evening flirting with the best man." She paused. "Why do you think there won't be a wedding?"

"There's something wrong. It happened the night of my grandmother's birthday party. All of a sudden he turned cool and remote. I think he's going to break up with me. He hasn't called me in two days."

"Oh, honey, this is normal," she said with a careless shrug. "Every man in love goes through it. It's what I call the seven-week itch. Only since you and Dylan were on the accelerated plan, it's more like the seventeen-day itch. That's the time when his bachelor friends are starting to plant subversive messages in his brain. They use words like 'hooked' and 'whipped' and make jokes about the ring in his nose. And they tell him that his life will never be the same."

"They do?"

"They do. But he'll get over it. And once he does, he won't be able to stay away from you. Especially if the sex was good. The sex was good, wasn't it?"

"It was incredible," Meggie admitted. "Are you sure he'll come back?"

"Do I know men?" Lana asked.

"Yes." Meggie replied, not really certain of her answer any more. "So what do I do?"

"Just be patient. And whatever you do, don't call him. Let him come to you."

"What if he never calls?"

"Oh, he'll call," Lana reassured her. "Just like he called that first time." She patted Meggie's shoulder. "You're a wonderful person. You're bright and funny and beautiful. And if Dylan Quinn can't see that, then he doesn't deserve you. And if things don't work out, we can always use the plan again on some other guy. With the revisions I've made, it should work even better than before."

Meggie turned back to her coffee. The prospect of going through this whole thing with another man was daunting at best. Besides, she'd already found the man she wanted, he just didn't want her.

The bell above the door jingled and Meggie watched glumly as the mailman walked in, his battered leather bag thrown over his shoulder, a transistor radio plugged into his ear. Lana hopped off her stool and hurried around to fetch him a cup of coffee as was her custom every day when he arrived. "So," she said. "What's new on Boylston Street, Roger? Any hot gossip?"

"I hear they're going to raise the rates on the parking meters," he said as he placed the stack of mail in front of Meggie. "And Berkley School of Music just put up new banners."

Meggie idly flipped through the envelopes, listening distractedly to Lana's conversation while she opened bills and notices. But her attention was diverted from the mail when she heard the word "firefighter." At first, she thought Lana was telling Roger the mailman about all her troubles. That's all Meggie needed was an opinion on her love life from a postal employee. But when she looked up, the stunned expression on Lana's face caused her heart to skip a beat.

"What?" she murmured.

"Roger just said the men from the Boylston Street station were called to a fire at about five this morning. They said on the radio that some firefighters from that station were injured."

Meggie blinked, the impact of Lana's words not hitting her right away. "It can't be him," she said. "He doesn't work nights."

"They were taken to Boston General," Roger said. "You can probably call the emergency room and find out who the guys were." He grabbed his coffee and gave them both a wave goodbye, leaving Meggie to worry about more than the bills he'd just delivered.

Injured? She'd never really thought about Dylan's job in terms of the danger he encountered. He always seemed so sure of himself, so confident in his abilities as a firefighter. But even Meggie knew that there were some situations where even the best firefighters met their match. "What should I do?" she murmured. She pushed off her stool. "I should call him at home. Or—or maybe I should call the hospital. But they probably won't give me any information over the phone."

Lana pushed her back down, then circled the counter to grab the phone. She paged through the phone book, then punched in a number. Meggie listened as she spoke but didn't really hear the words through the haze of worry. Dylan didn't work nights, he wouldn't have been at this fire. She glanced up as Lana put the phone back beneath the bar.

"I called the station house and asked for Dylan Quinn."

"If Dylan is hurt, I want to know." Meggie didn't want to wait by the phone for someone to call her and give her the bad news. Besides, who would think to call her? It wasn't as if she was his wife or a relative or even his girlfriend.

"All they said was that he's at the hospital. But that doesn't mean he was hurt."

"I'm going to go down there. To the hospital."

Meggie expected Lana to protest, but instead her partner quickly agreed. "Do you want me to drive you?"

"I have my car. I'll be fine" She took a ragged breath and tried to slow the pace of her heart. "He can't be hurt. He just can't be. I mean, I know his job is dangerous, but he always seemed so...invincible."

"Go," Lana urged. "And call me as soon as you find out anything."

Meggie ran out the front door to her car, parked at a meter in front of the shop. She hopped inside, then paused before she turned the ignition. She wasn't sure what kind of reception she'd get at the hospital, but it didn't make any difference. Once she was certain Dylan hadn't been hurt, then she could go home.

"I guess this is what it's like to be in love," she murmured, stunned by the revelation. She'd always dreamed of falling in love, finding a man who would turn her life upside down. But she'd never expected love to be a mixture of confusion and fear and dread. If Dylan was hurt, or even...Meggie swallowed hard. She didn't want to consider that possibility! He wasn't dead. He wasn't even hurt.

But one thought kept rolling around in her mind, one thought she couldn't abide. She might never get a chance to tell him how she really felt, never get a chance to say those three special words and really mean them. And that would be the greatest tragedy of all.

DYLAN GLANCED UP at the clock on the wall in the waiting room, watching the seconds tick by. Then he leaned back in his chair and closed his eyes. He and the rest of the firefighters from the Boylston Street station had come directly to the hospital from the fire. Two of their own had been injured, two men under Dylan's command—Artie Winton and Jeff Reilly. They'd been working on the second story of a burning warehouse when the floor gave way and they both fell through to the story below.

The strange thing was, they weren't even supposed to be there. One of the guys on the night shift had gotten married yesterday and Dylan's crew had offered to cover their shift so that some of the firefighters could attend the wedding and reception. They'd done a favor that had gone sour and now he was left to figure out why it had happened in the first place.

Getting information on their condition from the doctors had been nearly impossible, but that didn't keep Dylan from waiting, watching the clock and wondering why it wasn't him in that hospital bed instead of his two friends. *He'd* been the one to take them into that building. *He'd* thought it was safe. But it had been so dark and smoky and hard to see. If he'd known it was going to go down as it had, he would have—

Dylan cursed softly. Guilt had been plaguing him from the moment the accident had happened and he'd run it over and over in his head. What should he have done differently? The floor hadn't burned through. When they fell, they fell into smoke, not fire. But if fire hadn't weakened the floor, what had?

He opened his eyes and stared at the clock again, imagining the worst. When they'd pulled Artie out of the building, he'd had at least a broken leg and possibly a punctured lung. And Jeff had been unconscious with a head wound and cuts and scrapes on his face. Dylan kept telling himself that no news was good news, but after hours of waiting, even that didn't ring true anymore.

"Dylan?"

He opened his eyes, certain that he'd slipped into a dream for just a moment. But then, he slowly turned and found Meggie standing a few feet away. Her eyes glistened with tears and she bit her lower lip to keep it from trembling. "I...I heard about the fire," she said. "The news was on the radio. Lana called the fire station and they said you were here. I just wanted to make sure you were all right."

Dylan rose and stared at her for a long moment, trying to figure out why she'd come. He was exhausted and edgy and his first thought was to question whether this visit was part of her plan. He closed his eyes and took a deep breath, refusing to give voice to the accusation. She couldn't have predicted the fire and only a first-class manipulator would use it to her advantage. There were a lot of things about Meggie Flanagan that he didn't understand, but he knew she could never sink that low.

"I'm fine," he muttered. "I can't say the same about Artie and Jeff though." She came closer, then reached out and took his hand. Her touch sent a wave of warmth though his body and he felt the frustrations of the day ebb, the worry drain out of him. He wanted to pull her into his arms and bury his face in her silken hair, to breathe in her scent. "They won't tell us anything."

"How long have you been here?"

"A couple hours." He glanced around impatiently. "Damn it, why won't they tell us anything?"

Meggie gave his hand a squeeze. "I'll go see what I can find out. Why don't you sit back down? You look exhausted."

Dylan watched her as she walked over to the nurse's station. Even after everything he'd learned and everything he suspected, he was still glad to see her. She radiated a calm that he was in desperate need of right now.

She returned a few moments later and he didn't wait for her to offer her hand. Instead, he grabbed it and pressed his lips to her fingers. "The doctor is coming right out." Meggie hesitated. "Would you like me to stay?"

Dylan nodded. She sat down next to him, leaning back in her chair and staring up at the clock as she did. They didn't speak. Dylan didn't feel the need for words. Just having her near was enough.

He closed his eyes again and as soon as he did, an image of the accident flashed in his brain. But he didn't try to brush it aside. Instead, he calmly watched it, over and over, hoping for a clue to what had gone wrong. Doubts and confusion seemed to drag him down and he knew he wouldn't figure anything out until he got some rest. Right now, all he wanted was to curl up in a clean, soft bed with Meggie tucked in beside him and sleep until he couldn't sleep anymore.

Dylan felt her grip tighten on his hand and he opened his eyes to see a doctor moving toward the waiting room. He tried to read the doctor's expression and when he thought it was positive, Dylan told himself that he was only seeing what he wanted to see.

"Your buddies are going to be fine," the doctor announced, as the firefighters gathered around him. "Mr. Winton has a broken leg. We'll be taking him to surgery later this evening and we'll set it with a few screws. He also has a few broken ribs which were causing his breathing problems, but he should make a full recovery and be back on his feet in a few months. Mr. Reilly has a concussion but the CAT scan shows no swelling. He should be able to go home tomorrow evening. They're both resting and will be able to see visitors in the morning. I suggest the rest of you go home and get some sleep." With that, the doctor turned briskly and headed back down the hall.

The men from the Boylston Street station breathed a collective sigh of relief before breaking into smiles and slaps on the back. Dylan glanced down at Meggie and smiled. "Thanks," he murmured.

She reached up and clutched the sleeve of his jacket. "Why don't you let me take you home? I've got my car outside and you probably don't need to go back to the station. It sounds like you've had a long night."

Dylan nodded, then grabbed his helmet and followed her to the elevator. Suddenly, he felt as if the weight of the world had been lifted off his shoulders. Artie and Jeff were all right. And Meggie was here and he could talk to her. There had been a time when he'd kept his problems locked tightly inside where they could gnaw away at him. But he knew he could tell her everything and she'd understand—everything except how he really felt about her.

He'd looked into her eyes and had seen the concern there. The notion that she cared gave him hope—hope that those feelings went deeper than just worry over an acquaintance. The Meggie Flanagan who had come looking for him at the hospital wasn't the same Meggie Flanagan who'd neatly written "REVENGE" on the top of her plan. And he still couldn't convince himself that the Meggie he knew possessed an ounce of vindictiveness.

They reached her car and Dylan shrugged out of his bulky jacket and kicked off his boots before he got inside. He tossed them both in the rear seat with his helmet, then crawled in and laid his head back against the seat.

"Everything is going to be all right," she murmured when she'd settled on the driver's side.

He turned and looked over at her, smiling weakly. "I know."

Her fingers gripped the wheel but she didn't make a move to start the car. "Remember when you pulled me out of my shop and you yelled at me for worrying about my espresso maker? You said, 'Today is a good day. No one died.'" She turned to him and met his gaze squarely. "Today is a good day. Your friend's leg will mend and he'll be back to work in no time. And the doctor said that Jeff will be fine."

"I just wish I knew what happened," Dylan said. "There's no reason they should have been hurt."

"You will. Tomorrow you'll figure it all out and it will make sense. But for today, you just have to let it go."

Dylan reached over and wove his fingers through her hair, then drew her closer. His gaze fell on her lips and at first, he hesitated, not sure of how to approach her. But then, there was nothing left to do but kiss her. She sighed softly as his lips met hers and the taste of her washed away the bitter taste of smoke and confusion.

This was what it was supposed to be like. This was love, solid and true and unshakable. As the kiss grew more intense, all his suspicions and concerns dissolved and Dylan knew that nothing made any difference at all except this feeling...this kiss...this incredible warmth he felt in his heart.

For now, that was all he needed. As along as he had Meggie's love, even if it was only for a day, or a week, then everything would be all right.

THE KITCHEN IN Dylan's apartment was typical for a bachelor. He had an entire cupboard full of cereal, nearly every brand that contained more sugar than nutrients. The refrigerator held little more than milk, beer, a jar of mustard and some cheese that had gone fuzzy. When Meggie found bread and a can of soup, she decided to make Dylan her favorite comfort food—grilled cheese and tomato soup.

After she cut the mold from the cheese, there was just enough for a single sandwich. She mixed milk with the soup and stood at the stove, carefully tending both. A glance at her watch told her Dylan had been in the shower for nearly a half hour.

The temptation to join him there had teased at her brain. But though she'd done something as audacious as make love to him on a pool table, Meggie wasn't certain how he'd react if she stepped into the shower with him. She turned the notion over and over in her mind, thinking of all the delicious possibilities.

A frisson of desire shot through her as an image flashed in her mind—Dylan, naked and wet and hard with need. The water would wash over them and he'd press her back against the wall and draw her legs up around his waist and...Meggie swallowed hard. It was a long leap between tomato soup and uninhibited sex in a man's shower, she mused.

Yet the urge to repeat what they'd shared just a few nights ago was stronger than ever. Meggie had never considered herself a very sensual person yet all she could think about was the reality of smoothing her hands over Dylan's chest or pressing a kiss against his flat belly or running her fingers along his rigid desire. She could even recall his scent, the smell of soap and aftershave and hard work that was unmistakably male. And then there was his voice, whispering her name as he reached his climax.

Meggie cursed softly, then flipped off the burners to the stove. She found a clean plate for the sandwich and set the mug of soup next to the grilled cheese. Then she grabbed a cold beer from the refrigerator and wandered toward Dylan's bedroom.

She knocked softly, but when he didn't answer, Meggie pushed the door open. Steam from the shower hung heavy in the air and for a moment, she expected him to walk out of the bathroom, damp and naked. But then she looked over to the bed and found Dylan there, stretched out on top of the covers, wearing only his boxer shorts, sound asleep.

A smile curled her lips and she softly approached. She set the soup and sandwich and beer down on the bedside table, but she couldn't bring herself to wake him. He looked so relaxed, the tension that she'd seen in his expression now gone. With a hesitant hand, she reached out to brush a damp lock of hair from his forehead.

He didn't stir, so Meggie knelt down beside the bed and studied him for a long time. She'd never noticed the small scar on his upper lip or how perfectly straight his nose was. And his jaw, such a determined angle to it. A man didn't have any right to be so beautiful.

She leaned closer, then gave into impulse and brushed a

soft kiss across his lips. When she pulled back and opened her eyes, she found him staring at her, his gaze fixed on hers. Meggie forced a smile. "I brought you some soup," she murmured. "And a sandwich."

But instead of thanking her, he reached out and slipped his hand through the hair at her nape and pulled her forward. His mouth met hers and almost immediately she tasted the need in his kiss. It was as if he were frantic to possess her, demanding that she respond.

Meggie moaned softly and tried to stand, but instead, she tumbled down on top of him, then rolled across the bed until she was beneath him. Desire raced through her, her reaction to his touch swift and stirring. Dylan tugged at her clothes, as anxious to feel skin against skin as she suddenly was.

This was no gentle seduction. It was raw and powerful and the need surged inside of Meggie until she thought she'd go out of her mind if she didn't feel him moving inside of her. He took her face between his hands and kissed her roughly, then drew her up until she knelt in front of him on the bed. Her sweater was the first to go and he yanked it over her head and carelessly tossed it aside. Then he reached for the bottom hem of her cotton camisole and pulled that over her head as well.

Dylan paused for a moment, smoothing his hands over her bare breasts, cupping them in his palms. But it wasn't enough and he fumbled with the button on her jeans. Meggie knew that he wanted her as much as she wanted him. His erection pressed against the front of his boxers. But rather than touch him, she pushed off the bed and stood next to it.

He watched her through half-hooded eyes as she slid her jeans down over her hips and kicked off her shoes and socks along with them. Then, she slipped out of her panties. When she stood naked in front of him, his gaze raked over her body. A tiny shiver skittered down her spine as she anticipated the next move, the move that would send her senses spinning out of control.

It came quickly. Dylan reached out and wrapped his arm around her waist, then pulled her back onto his bed and back beneath his body. Meggie stretched out along the length of him, his desire pressing between her legs, probing at her entrance. She ached for the sensation of him entering her without any barriers between them. But though he'd lost all contact with common sense, Meggie knew better.

She furrowed her hands through his hair and gently drew his damp mouth away from hers. Dylan groaned softly and stole one more kiss before opening his eyes. It was as if he could see right to her soul. He reached over to the bedside table and grabbed a box in the top drawer, then placed it in her hand without saying a word.

As she slipped the condom over him, he watched her, as if the act was more a caress than a matter of practicality. And when she was finished, she tossed the box and wrapper aside.

A moment later, he was above her and then inside her. Their joining was primitive, raw with need and almost violent in its intensity. He couldn't seem to get close enough, couldn't seem to fill her completely, his need insatiable, his mood driven. Meggie arched beneath him until she felt him deep in her core and he sighed raggedly.

She wanted this as much as he did, this mindless coupling. It drove away all her doubt and guilt, leaving pure emotion in its wake. She loved Dylan Quinn, that was all that she knew. She loved him with her heart and her mind and yes, her body. And nothing could change that. But this is what she needed right now, this exquisite pleasure she took in his body and he took in hers.

As she rose toward her climax, sensation pulsing through her, Meggie heard him murmur her name. It was like a cry for help and a plea for release, and a promise that he would be with her when she fell. And then Meggie felt herself swell around him and a tremor raced through her. The first spasm came as a shock, but then they rolled over her like waves on a beach, warm and delicious. An instant later, he joined her, tensing at first, then exploding inside her with a low groan.

When they both came back to earth, Dylan rolled to her side and curled her body against his. His breath slowed and for a moment, Meggie thought he might be asleep. But then he spoke, his breath soft against her ear. "Don't ever leave me," he murmured. "Promise me."

"I won't," Meggie said. But the promise cost dearly. Though she never wanted to leave him, that didn't mean that he wouldn't someday send her away. Or that she would choose to leave on her own. Nothing assured them of a future together. Great sex didn't magically turn into a lifelong commitment.

Meggie rolled over in his arms and stared at his face in the soft light. He slept soundly, peacefully, their joining driving away the demons that had nagged at him since the fire. She reached out and smoothed her hand over his cheek. "I love you," she murmured, the words coming out on a soft breath. "I can't help myself. I've always loved you and I always will."

But her feelings, however deep, wouldn't change the fact that she'd somehow tricked him into wanting her. All men want what they can't have, Lana had told her. How long would Dylan want her once he knew she could refuse him nothing? She'd already seen that faraway look in his eyes, felt the sting of indifference in his words. The first signs were there.

Meggie slowly wriggled out of his arms, then knelt next to him on the bed. The prospect of seeing that look again, especially after their passionate time together would be enough to break her heart into a million pieces. So rather than spend the night and dread the morning, she'd retreat and leave him to sleep alone.

And when he woke up, maybe he'd wonder whether he'd possessed her at all. Maybe he'd believe it was just a dream. And then maybe he'd come back just once more.

Meggie brushed an errant tear from her cheek then crawled out of the bed and began to gather her clothes. She dressed slowly, all the while watching him. When she was finally through, Meggie couldn't bear to make herself leave without touching him just once more. She walked to the bed and gently placed her palm on his heart. It beat slow and strong beneath her fingers.

Then, with a ragged sigh, she turned and walked out of the room. And when she reached her car parked on the street in front of his building she paused. Though she fought the urge to return to his arms and his bed, Meggie knew this was for the best. She needed time to figure out her next move, time to find a way to make him love her for real. And she couldn't concentrate when he looked into her eyes or touched her.

Meggie unlocked her car, then took one last look up at Dylan's bedroom window. She imagined him still curled up, his limbs tangled in the sheets. Someday, maybe she'd be able to stay. Someday, maybe his bed would be hers as well.

But today wasn't that day.

8

SHE WAS GONE when he woke up at dusk. Dylan rolled over in his empty bed, then moaned softly. He wasn't surprised. Hell, nothing Meggie did surprised him anymore. Not her stalwart support at the hospital, not her gentle concern when they got back to his apartment. And not even her uninhibited passion in his arms as they made love.

Now that he understood her motives, everything fell perfectly into place. Making love to him hadn't been about the two of them, it had been about her little plan for revenge, about reeling him in and turning his need for her against him.

Dylan closed his eyes and threw his arm over his face, wishing that he could block it all out of his brain. She must have a heart of ice to use him so completely, then cast him aside. But no matter how he tried to reconcile the two Meggies he knew, Dylan still came up short. He'd looked into her eyes at the very moment he'd entered her and he'd seen emotion there, passion and ecstasy, and yes, love. If she was faking it, then she was a better actress than any Academy Award winner.

He rolled over and grabbed his shirt from where he'd tossed it earlier that day. It still smelled faintly of smoke. The paper was still there, tucked in his breast pocket, a reminder of everything that was wrong between him and Meggie Flanagan. Dylan pulled it out and scanned the diagram. Over and over again, he'd tried to attach an alternate meaning to what he saw. After all, how could she possibly harbor such ill feelings over something as stupid as a high-school dance.

He raked his hand through his hair. Unless, of course, she was a psycho. A bitter laugh burst from his lips. He could attribute many qualities to Meggie, but deranged wasn't one of them. "So what the hell is this all about?" Dylan murmured, staring down at her plan.

With a soft curse, he glanced around the room, his gaze falling on the tangled sheets of his bed. An image flashed in his mind, Meggie naked, her skin flushed with desire, her mouth damp from his kisses. She was everything he'd ever wanted in a woman. But he didn't want this—the doubt, the confusion, the anger. He'd had enough.

Dylan tossed the paper on the bed, then quickly rummaged through his closet, looking for a clean pair of jeans and a shirt that wasn't too wrinkled. This had gone on long enough and it was time to put an end to it. If Meggie really loved him, then he'd force her to admit it. And if she didn't, then he'd walk away.

He shoved the paper into his pocket and shrugged into his jacket on the way out. Dylan wasn't sure what he planned to say to her, but it wasn't going to be pretty. For the first time in his life, he'd risked everything and fallen in love. And this is where it had got him. "Maybe I should have listened more closely to all those tales of the Mighty Quinns," he muttered as he tossed his helmet, jacket and boots into the trunk of his car.

What had ever made him think he could find a relationship like Conor and Olivia's? He wasn't cut out for happily-ever-after and he shouldn't have deluded himself into believing otherwise.

Dylan reached for the radio and flipped it on. The blaring sounds of Aerosmith and the play-by-play of a Patriots game didn't drown out the constant questions, the unrelenting regret. He wondered if someday, a young Quinn ancestor would hear how the mighty Dylan Quinn had fallen under the spell of the beautiful Meggie Flanagan and how she'd stomped on his heart and left him weak and powerless.

A frown creased his brow. For that to happen, there would have to be ancestors. And if the Quinn brothers never found love, then that wasn't going to happen. And if they did, they wouldn't have any reason to pass on those ridiculous tales! "You're not thinking straight," he muttered. "Just keep your eye on the ball and don't let her draw you in again."

He parked at the station and returned his gear to the alcove. Then, as he walked the distance to Meggie's shop, he went over what he wanted to say. He'd just lay it all on the line, admit his feelings for her and demand complete honesty in return. If she wanted him, so be it. And if she didn't, then he was willing to walk away. But all his resolve wavered the moment he walked into Cuppa Joe's.

Meggie was standing at the cash register, her expression intense. She looked like she'd just crawled out of his bed, her hair mussed and her lips still swollen from his kisses. She punched at the buttons, then cursed, then punched them again before she looked up. Dylan held his breath, ready to read her reaction. Would she pretend to be happy to see him? Or would she offer some lame apology for sneaking out without a word?

He didn't bother to wait. Instead, he strode up to the counter and slammed the piece of paper onto the copper surface with the flat of his hand. "Just get it over with," he demanded, his jaw tight, his temper barely under control.

Meggie gasped, taken aback by his sudden appearance and by the tone in his voice. "What?"

Dylan shook his head. "Don't play coy with me, Meggie. I know what you're up to. It's all here, in your little plan."

She stared down at the paper in disbelief. Hesitantly, she reached out and took it. Stunned recognition dawned on her face. "Where did you find this?" she asked.

"Never mind where I found it."

"I—I don't know what to say." She pushed it back toward him. "You weren't supposed to see that. It doesn't mean anything."

"Just tell me it's over," Dylan demanded, his heart pounding so hard he could hear it in his head. "Or maybe it can't be over until I admit that I love you." He drew a deep breath, his angry gaze fixed on her. "All right, here it is. I love you. I love you more than I've ever loved a woman before. Hell, I don't think I *have* loved a woman before you. You're the first. Does that make you feel good? Because, for a while there it made me feel real good." He cursed softly. "But now it makes me feel kind of stupid."

Meggie reached out to touch his hand, but he pulled it away. "I'm sorry," she said. "But you don't understand. This was never meant to—"

"Hurt me?" Dylan interrupted. "Well, it did. And I think in the end, it hurt you, too. Because we could have had something really great. Only you can't see that."

"We do have something great," she said.

"We have something weird and kind of sick."

"No! It's not like that," Meggie protested. "Lana and I put that plan together that first night you came in here. It was silly and I didn't take it seriously. But, then when you called me up for a date, I didn't know what to do. I don't have a lot of experience with men, Dylan, at least not a lot of experience that prepared me for you. So I decided to follow the plan."

"Do you really expect me to believe this? Everything that happened between us was right there on this paper. From your four-day waiting period until accepting a date to the invitation to your grandmother's birthday party. Even those flowers from David were a lie."

"Lana sent the flowers. And I didn't invite you to that party, you invited yourself."

"And it's a good thing I did, because if I hadn't, I never would have figured out what you were up to. Your brother was the one who gave me the heads-up. He told me about the Sophomore Frolic and how you expected me to take you instead of Brian."

She stared at him for a long while and he could see the pain and regret in her eyes. Dylan wanted to take the words back, to simply pull her into his arms and erase all the anger with a flurry of kisses. But he couldn't touch her. Once he did, he knew he'd be lost.

"I was wrong," Meggie said. "I misunderstood. And by the time I found out, that stupid plan was already history."

"I thought what we had was real. And now I find out that it was all just a game to you."

"It started as a game, but it didn't end that way," Meggie insisted. "I never expected you to ask me out again after that first date and when you did, I wasn't sure what to do. I just figured, why not use the plan? I knew, sooner or later, you'd move on to someone else, so it didn't make a difference."

Dylan wasn't sure how to respond. He'd wanted to believe that Meggie was different, that what they shared was real. And maybe there were real emotions at work here, but they'd been tainted by her deceit and manipulation.

"I know you, Dylan. I've watched you since I was thirteen. I'm not the kind of girl you want. And you may think you love me, but that's just because the plan worked. It'll wear off after a while."

Her words cut right to the quick and though he knew she didn't mean to be cruel, he couldn't help his own reaction. There it was. It all came back to the same thing—his reputation, his charm and the long list of ladies he'd bedded. His feelings for Meggie didn't make a bit of difference as long as he was carrying around all that old baggage.

But hadn't he proved himself to her? What did she want that he hadn't given her? He certainly couldn't change the past. If he could, he would have. But this was who he was. A surge of anger raced through him. He'd accepted her past and hadn't let it affect their future, why couldn't she accept him, warts and all?

"Maybe you're right," Dylan murmured. Maybe he had been caught up in a fantasy that could never become reality. He'd wanted to believe that he could find a woman to love, just like Conor had. But he wasn't Conor and he never could be. "I have to go," he said. He stared at her long and hard, unable to believe that this was the end of it. He'd admitted he loved her and now he had to walk away.

"I never meant to hurt you," Meggie said, her voice soft and tremulous. "And I'm sorry if I did."

Though her apologies made a fitting end to their conversation, they didn't make Dylan feel any better. He turned and strode toward the door. He was tempted to look back, but his pride wouldn't allow it. Meggie had wandered in and out of his life once before and he'd forgotten her.

He could do it again. Only this time, Dylan suspected it would take a lot longer for the memories to fade.

"YA LOOK LIKE yer in a desperate state," Seamus Quinn muttered. "Here, drink yer Guinness and buck up, boyo. Life can't be that bad, can it?"

Dylan pushed aside his empty beer bottle, then grabbed the Guinness and took a hearty gulp. If he drank enough it might dull his senses. And if he managed that, then he might be able to forget about Meggie Flanagan and their brief, but passionate, affair.

"So, tell me," Seamus asked. "Are you acting the *gom* over a woman? Or is it something else?"

The last person Dylan wanted to discuss his love life with was Seamus Quinn. He didn't need *I-told-you-so*s on top of everything else he was feeling. Hell, he'd heaped enough of that on himself. "Nah, there's nothing wrong, Da. Just worried over my buddies at work."

"Those lads who got themselves injured in that fire? So how are they, then?"

"They're good," Dylan said. "Winton will get out of the hospital in a few days and Reilly goes home tomorrow. They should be back on the job before too long." He picked up his Guinness then slid back from the bar. "I'm going to see what Brendan is up to," he murmured.

His brother was sitting in a booth near the pool table, papers spread all over the table, and a half-eaten bowl of Irish stew next to his laptop computer. "Can I sit down?" Dylan asked.

Brendan glanced up, then shoved his papers aside. "Sure. I didn't realize you were here. When did you come in?"

"A few minutes ago."

"I heard about the fire," Brendan said, eyeing him shrewdly. "Some of your crew stopped in here on their way home. They said you left the hospital with Meggie. So what are you doing here?"

"Well, I needed a beer. A few beers. In fact, I think I'll drink so many beers that I won't be able to see straight. So," Dylan said, nodding toward the stacks of papers. "What are you working on?"

"An article for *Adventure* magazine. It's about that trip I took on the Amazon last spring. And some of this is for my book." Brendan reached out and tried to straighten the mess. "I need an assistant," he said. "I've got so much stuff to put together and it's all on little scraps of paper. Interview notes on cocktail napkins, phone numbers on matchbooks. I have to get organized or I'll never get this book—" Brendan stopped. "Are you even listening to me?"

Dylan glanced up, then nodded. "Yeah. Little scraps of paper. That's a problem."

Brendan chuckled softly. "So, you had a fight with Meggie?"

Dylan hadn't really wanted to talk about his problems, but now that Brendan brought it up, he realized that it might be good to get a second viewpoint on what went on. "Naw, not a fight. It's just over." He shook his head, then took another sip of beer. "I don't know what made me think it would ever work. I've never had a committed relationship in my life. Why should I start now?"

"Because you're in love with her, you stupid *gobdaw*. Anyone can see that."

"Is it that obvious?" Dylan asked.

"Only to your brothers. The rest of the world probably just thinks that look on your face is from a bad case of constipation. That or your underwear is creeping."

"She made up this plan to get me to fall in love with her just so she could dump me. All for something she thinks I did way back in high school."

"I know. Con told me all about it."

Dylan gasped. "What? Is my love life the hot topic of conversation at Quinn's Pub?"

"Yeah, maybe. There's not much else to talk about except for Con's wedding and I've had about enough of that. I never thought I'd see the day when he got so excited over table linens and china patterns. The poor guy has gone completely 'round the bend. I'm thinking we should stage one of those interventions."

"He hasn't gone 'round the bend," Dylan said. "In fact, I know how he feels. It's easy to be excited about those things when the woman you love is excited about them. When Meggie talked about her coffee shop, I could listen all night while she chattered on about French roast and Italian roast and how it's important to get the steamed milk to precisely the right temperature. When she talked about things like that, her whole face lit up and she looked more beautiful than she'd ever looked before."

"God, you are in love, aren't you," Brendan said, leaning back to stare at him in disbelief.

"Yeah, that's the real corker. I don't know whether to be angry or hurt or whether I should do a little happy jig on the bar. She wanted me to fall in love with her and I did. I'm in love and there's not a thing I can do about it. I said the words, but she doesn't believe me, because, of course, I'm Dylan Quinn and I can't possibly fall in love. I'm simply not capable of feeling that emotion."

"Well, you've made a mess of it, I can see," Brendan said. "I suppose you and Con are going to be lording this over the rest of us."

"Don't look so disgusted. You'll have your day and it's probably coming a lot sooner than you think," Dylan warned.

"Conor started something in this family, maybe not intentionally. But he showed us all the possibilities. He proved that all those silly Mighty Quinn stories don't have to be true. And sooner or later, you're going to want what he has. And what I almost had."

"Past tense?"

"Very past tense," Dylan murmured.

"You don't sound convinced."

Dylan took another sip of his Guinness. "I'm not. It used to be so easy to forget a woman. I just moved on to someone else. But how the hell am I supposed to forget Meggie? It's like she burrowed her way into my heart and she's not leaving any time soon. I should be mad as hell that she manipulated me, yet I have to believe that what went on between us was real. I wasn't wrong about that."

"So, let's lay it on the line," Brendan said. "You told her you loved her and she didn't believe you. She didn't return the sentiment, but chances are she feels the same way. The way I look at it, all you have to do is convince her that you can't live without her and that she can't live without you. That shouldn't be too hard."

"I don't know. I don't think I can go back there."

"Are you really angry about what Meggie said and did or are you just using this as an excuse?"

Dylan had to admit that the idea had crossed his mind more than once. What Meggie did really wasn't that bad. She'd wanted him to fall in love with her and he had. And she'd made no move to dump him, to exact her revenge. He'd been the one to dump her.

"You should get out while you still can. Avoid the inevitable—a lifetime of happiness with the woman you love."

Dylan sighed, then shook his head. "I don't want to get out, but I just don't know how to fix this. Usually, whenever I had a problem with a woman, that signalled the end of the relationship. I've never really had to work at it. And don't know if Meggie feels the same way about me as I do about her. I think she does, but then I haven't been the best judge of the truth in this relationship. I just wish we could start all over again. You know, a fresh start, from the beginning. That way I'd be certain it was real." Dylan stared morosely into his glass.

"I know what will help you," Brendan said. "A nice round of darts."

"I don't feel like playing."

"Aw, now don't be givin' me that sad puss," Brendan said in a thick Irish brogue. He leaned forward, bracing his elbows on the table. "You want my advice?"

"Isn't that what you've been giving me for the past ten minutes?"

"No, that was just conversation. Listen carefully, brother, because this is advice."

Dylan held up his hand. "To be honest, I'd rather get Olivia's advice. She'd know what I should do. She knows a lot about how women think, more than you do."

"You insult me, lad," Brendan said. "I know exactly what you should do and I'll tell you."

"So tell me."

"If you want to go back to the beginning and start again, then do it. There's nothing to stop you."

"My time machine is in the shop," Dylan muttered.

"Be creative. Think outside the box. Do something unexpected." Brendan slid out of the booth, then gave Dylan a slap on the back. "Come on, I'll let you win at darts. That should make you feel better."

"Let me win?" Dylan said. "You haven't beaten me at darts in five years."

Dylan grudgingly slid out of the booth and walked toward the back of the bar. Maybe a rousing round of darts would take his mind off his troubles with Meggie. But he knew as soon as he was alone again, they'd all come flooding back.

As he plucked the darts from the dartboard, Dylan's thoughts wandered back to Brendan's advice. An idea began to form in his mind, a way to turn back the clock. He put his toe on the line painted on the floor and tossed a dart at the board. It stuck just a few inches short of the bull's-eye.

Maybe the idea would work, he mused. But something like this would take a plan. A very detailed plan.

"IT'S OVER," Meggie said, staring into her cup of coffee as if it might offer some answers. But she knew there were no answers to her problems. Nothing she said or did could repair the damage that had been done and now she was left to live with the consequences. "I should never have agreed to that plan. I should have thrown it out the minute you put pen to paper."

"I'm sorry," Lana said. "This is all my fault. Maybe I

should go over to the firehouse and explain it all to Dylan. It's been three days and he's probably had a chance to cool off. Besides, he can't hold you responsible for something that I did, can he? I mean, the handwriting on that paper isn't even yours."

"That's not the point," Meggie said. "The plan worked. But in the end, it didn't work."

"I don't understand."

"He told me he loved me." Meggie's voice wavered slightly as she said the words, remembering the moment she heard them. Though he'd declared his love in anger, it still didn't erase the joy she felt. Dylan Quinn had fallen in love with her. And she'd fallen in love with him. And that, in itself, was a miracle.

"I thought when a man finally said that to me, my life would change forever. I thought I'd be picking out a wedding dress and deciding what to name my first child. But my life hasn't changed at all. I'm back to where I was the day Dylan carried me out of the shop."

"If you truly love him, Meggie, and he truly loves you, then things will work out."

"That only happens in fairy tales. I think he realizes that I never meant to reach the revenge part of the plan. He's just using that as an excuse. The little alarm bell went off in his head and now it's time for him to move on. Maybe it's time for me to move on, too."

"Don't say that," Lana cried. "You're in love and you shouldn't give up so easily."

"But everything is so messed up! How am I going to straighten this out?"

Lana thought about the question for a long moment, then smiled. "Where is the plan?" she asked.

Meggie slipped off her stool and circled the counter to retrieve the crumpled paper that Dylan had tossed in her face. She also grabbed the notebook where they'd scribbled their early strategies and the computer printout of Lana's latest revision. She handed them all to Lana. "Take them. I don't ever want to look at them again."

"I think we should get rid of it all, right now," Lana said.

"Good idea," Meggie cried.

Lana hopped off her stool, scooped up the papers and notebook and headed toward the office. "Well, are you coming?"

Meggie frowned, then hurried after her. "Where are you going?" By the time Meggie reached the office, Lana had brought out the metal trash can from beneath the desk and dumped its contents in the corner of the office. She then placed the trash can in the center of the tiny room.

With a grand flourish, she handed Meggie the notebook. "Go ahead," she said. "Tear it to bits and throw it away."

When Meggie had shredded the notebook, Lana leaned over the can and spit. "That's for all those men who don't know a good woman when they find one."

"Damn straight," Meggie added as she spit into the trash can.

Lana held up the computer report and Meggie snatched it from her fingers and tore into it. When she'd finished, she dumped it on top of the scraps from the notebook. "That felt really good," she murmured. "Give me something else." The computer disk was next and Meggie did her best to dismantle it before adding it to the pile.

Then, the only thing left was the crumpled paper that Dylan had found. But as Lana handed it to her, she smiled slyly. "Don't throw that away yet. Since he touched it, since he put his eyes on this very private piece of paper, I have something special planned." She reached into her pocket and withdrew a lighter and before Meggie could protest, Lana lit the corner of the paper on fire.

Meggie cried out as it flamed, then dropped it into the trash can on top of the other papers. "Are you crazy?"

"It's a metal trash can," Lana said. "It'll burn out in a few seconds."

But it didn't burn out. In fact, the contents began to smoke, the plastic from the computer disk causing an acrid smell. Meggie frantically searched for something to put out the fire. She grabbed Lana's jacket from behind the door, but Lana yanked it out of her arms. "That's cashmere," her partner cried. "Six hundred dollars."

"Well, we need to find something to put this out before the alarm goes off!"

Just as she said the words, a piercing sound split the air. She grabbed the phone, determined to catch it before the system automatically called the fire department, but it was too late. With a soft curse, she hurried to the counter and grabbed the fire extinguisher they'd purchased after the last fire. But by the time she reached the office, the fire had burned itself out. All that was left was smoke and some charred paper. She dropped the extinguisher on the floor.

Her partner leaned on the edge of her desk, the same sly smile curling her lips that was there when she suggested this little ritual. Realization suddenly dawned. "You did this on purpose!" Meggie cried. "You knew the plastic from that computer disk would start smoldering and set off the alarm."

Lana looked at her watch. "Dylan should be rolling up any minute now. I called the firehouse just to make sure he was on duty. If I were you I'd comb my hair and dab on a little lipstick. You look a little frazzled."

Meggie cursed out loud, then spun around to look at her reflection in the mirror on the wall. Though she hadn't spent much time getting ready that morning, she wasn't having such a bad day. She pinched her cheeks and ran her fingers through her hair, then pressed her hand to her heart.

She wasn't sure whether she really wanted to see him or not. When he'd left the shop a few days ago, he'd been so angry. She had to prepare herself for the worst, the prospect that he might walk in and not even speak to her.

Meggie and Lana stood in the middle of the shop and waited, the unused fire extinguisher at their feet. A few minutes later, a trio of firemen strode through the door. Meggie's heart fell when she saw that Dylan was one of them. But he stood back, near the door and sent the other two ahead.

"The fire is out," Lana said. "It was in the office. I'll show you the way." Lana gave her a wide-eyed smile as she tagged after Dylan's two handsome co-workers. When they'd disappeared into the rear of the shop, Meggie had no choice but to acknowledge Dylan's presence.

"Hi," she murmured. He looked so handsome in his firefighter gear, so strong and resolute. Her knees went weak as his gaze met hers.

He nodded curtly, then glanced down at the floor. "I see you got a fire extinguisher."

"It was just a little fire," Meggie said. "It went out almost as quickly as it began. Besides, I couldn't figure out how to work it."

He sighed softly. "Set it in front of you on the floor," he instructed, "like this." He took her hand and wrapped her fingers around the handle, then covered her hand with his. "Pull the pin, squeeze and the foam will come out."

"Thanks." She swallowed hard in a feeble attempt to control the tremor in her voice. Her mind wandered back to the time they'd spent in his bed, the passion they'd shared, her shattering response to his touch. Even now, she could still recall the feel of his hands against her skin.

"How did it start?" Dylan asked, his voice cool and efficient, the perfect firefighter.

Though she could barely maintain her composure around him, he wasn't having the same trouble around her. "Lana," Meggie said. "She dropped a match into the trash can by mistake and the trash caught on fire."

Dylan glanced over her shoulder and she turned to watch the two firemen emerge from the office, one of them carrying the trash can. He brought it to Dylan. Reaching in, Dylan picked out the charred remains of the notebook. Then he pulled out a half-burned flowchart. He raised his eyebrow as he held the paper out to Meggie. "This looks familiar."

She opened her mouth to speak, but then at the last minute, changed her mind. Nothing she could say would help. He believed he'd been manipulated and he had the proof in his hands. He probably even thought that she'd set the fire herself, just to lure him back.

"Do you have a few minutes?" she asked. "I'd like to talk to you. Privately."

Dylan grabbed the trash can from his co-worker's arms. "Why don't you guys wait outside. Let Carmichael know I'll be done in here in a few minutes."

The pair walked outside. Meggie wondered how long Lana was planning to stay in the office and whether she'd have time to say what she needed to say. She took a deep breath, then hardened her resolve. She'd only have one chance and she planned on making sure he didn't walk out of Cuppa Joe's with any doubts about her feelings.

"What did you want to talk about?" Dylan murmured.

"Don't rush me," she murmured. "I have to say this right." She looked up at him, meeting his gaze squarely. "I love you." The words came out as if they were all one word. Meggie took another breath. "I—love—you. There. Now you know how I feel. I don't expect that it will change anything, but I just wanted you to know that you weren't the only one with feelings here."

Dylan stared at her, a slight frown wrinkling his brow. His mouth dropped open slightly and for a moment, she thought she saw surprise in his expression.

"I know you probably don't believe me, but I don't care. Making that plan was stupid and I know there's no way I can change the past. But I thought you deserved to hear the truth and that's it."

She took a shaky breath and waited for him to speak. But the bell on the door snapped him back to reality. Meggie turned to see one of the firefighters at the entrance to the shop. "We just got a call. Auto accident a couple blocks away. There's fuel on the street."

Dylan nodded, then turned his attention back to Meggie. His gaze probed hers, as if searching for the truth of her words. "I have to go."

"Yes," she said.

"I don't know what to say."

"You don't have to say anything. I understand."

He turned to walk toward the door, then stopped and looked back at her. For a moment, she thought he might stride right back to her, yank her into his arms and kiss her. But then, he glanced over his shoulder at his buddies waiting outside. "I'll see you."

"I'll see you," Meggie said.

Meggie stared numbly at the door as it swung shut. She had wanted to put the Frolic fiasco behind her, to banish it from her memory along with Dylan Quinn. And instead, she just made new memories to replace the old, new regrets and new heartaches. She'd poured out her heart to him, said all the words she thought he wanted to hear and he'd simply turned and walked away.

A few seconds later, Lana emerged from the office. She

stood next to Meggie and draped her arm around her shoulder. "So it didn't go well?"

"I told him I loved him. And then he walked out. No, I'd have to say that wasn't the reaction I was hoping for." She paused. "Although, he didn't say goodbye. He said he'd see me. That's kind of hopeful, isn't it?"

Meggie wandered back to the counter and sat down on a stool. She loved Dylan Quinn. Not in the silly schoolgirl way she'd loved him in high school. This love was soul-deep and part of who she was. And now that she had said the words, she felt better, as if she'd been released from all the deceit and manipulation.

"You told him," Lana said. "And that's good. You gave him something to think about. And once he does, he'll be back."

"How do you know?"

Lana sighed. "I know men. What can I say? It's a gift."

Meggie wanted to believe her. And she wanted to believe that Dylan meant what he'd said just a few days ago. For if he really loved her and she really loved him, then, in the end, nothing should keep them apart.

9

"SMILE. SAY 'MAJOR profit potential'!"

Lana slipped her arm around Meggie's waist and smiled at the camera. Meggie held up a Cuppa Joe's coffee mug and Kristine snapped a picture.

"Just one more," she said. "Meggie, you need to smile! This is an exciting day!"

This was the day they'd been waiting for since she and Lana had graduated from business school, the day they'd talked about over take-out pizza and dirty laundry and stock market investment strategies. And now that it was here, Meggie couldn't seem to work up a good case of enthusiasm. Something was missing and she suspected it was Dylan.

This was the biggest event in her professional life and she wanted Dylan to share it with her. Since he'd responded to the ceremonial fire in her office, she hadn't heard from him. Meggie had thought about calling, but this time, she believed in Lana's admonitions. The ball was in his court; he had to make the next move.

Lana had tried her best to cheer Meggie up over the past few days. She brought her special treats, doughnuts in the morning and a sinful cheeseburger for lunch. One night, she'd even treated Meggie to a manicure. In turn, Meggie had vowed that the day of the grand opening would be the last day Dylan Quinn would invade her thoughts. There were so many other things to occupy her mind than regrets. Yet she knew, in those secret hours while she waited for sleep to come, unbidden images of Dylan would swim in her head and she'd be transported back to the night on the pool table or that morning in his bed.

"Hold the mug out a little further," Kristine directed as she snapped another photo.

They'd hired eight employees, Kristine being the most experienced. She'd been named assistant manager and would lessen the workload for Meggie and Lana. And her boyfriend was active in the local music scene and had promised to help book singers as soon as business took off.

Danielle, a college student from Boston University, was also working the counter. She'd come to them from Starbucks and knew the ins and outs of the espresso maker better than Eddie from the restaurant supply house. She could steam milk to the perfect temperature without using a thermometer and she could mix four different coffee drinks at once, keeping all the flavors and options straight in her head. Two more workers were scheduled to come on at 4:00 and since they'd decided to open at 9:00 instead of the usual 7:00 a.m., today would be a short day.

"Now, I think I need to get a photo of you two bringing out the sign," Kristine suggested.

Meggie and Lana hurried back inside the shop and dragged out the heavy sandwich sign that would sit at the edge of the sidewalk, proclaiming the shop open. They posed once more, then Lana glanced at her watch. "I think it's time," she said.

Her excitement was infectious and Meggie returned her smile. "This is it," she said. "This is what we've been saving for all this time." A tiny shiver coursed through her body. "I'm a little scared."

They walked back inside, arm in arm and flipped on the neon coffee cups that adorned the front windows. Then they stood behind the counter and waited...and waited...and waited.

They were open nearly an hour before the first customer walked inside, a delivery man carrying a huge box under his arm. Meggie stepped up to the register and smiled. The rest of the staff waited expectantly, Kristine with the camera, ready to catch the first money that crossed the counter. "Welcome to Cuppa Joe's," Meggie said. "What can I get for you?"

"Just a signature," he said, holding out a clipboard. "I've got a delivery here for Meggie Flanagan. Is that you?"

Congratulatory gifts had been arriving all week. There were more beautiful plants scattered throughout the shop and gleaming plaques from the local business associations declaring them members of the Greater Boston Chamber of Commerce and the Back Bay Retailers and the Boylston Street Neighborhood Cooperative. Meggie took the box and set it on the counter. It didn't have a return address, it was simply wrapped in brown paper and tied with a string. She tore the paper off and pulled the lid from the box, then pushed back a layer of tissue paper.

On top was an envelope, but it was what lay beneath that caused the most curiosity. The gift was made of fabric, some type of satiny material in a shade of Pepto-Bismol pink. Meggie dropped the card on the counter and pulled the fabric out only to realize that she'd been sent a dress—a floor-length, formal dress.

"What the hell is that?" Lana asked.

"I'm not sure," Meggie said. "But it looks like—" She paused. "Oh my God, it can't be."

"What?"

"It's the formal I wore to the Sophomore Frolic." She turned it around and looked at the back. The big bow was there right where it had been all those years ago. "It's the exact same dress. Where did this come from? I had this packed away in my closet at my parents' house." Meggie pushed aside the tissue paper to find a pair of shoes dyed to match the awful pink color. "I can't believe I actually wore this. I thought it looked so cool, like the dress Madonna wore in that 'Material Girl' video. Never mind that it was already four or five years out of date."

"Why would your mother send you an old formal?"

"I don't know," Meggie said. She reached for the card, but as she opened the vellum envelope, she realized it wasn't a card at all but a hand-lettered invitation. "The Sophomore Class of South Boston High cordially invites you to attend the Sophomore Frolic, held tonight in the gymnasium of South

Boston High School. A limousine will pick you up promptly at 8:00 p.m."

Lana grabbed the invitation from Meggie's fingers and read it aloud all over again. Then she grinned. "It's from him," she said excitedly.

"Dylan?" Meggie asked. "Why would he do this? Is this some kind of joke?"

"No! It's a grand romantic gesture," Lana explained. "He's planning to sweep you off your feet."

"Dressed in this formal?" Meggie asked.

"Don't you see? He wants to take you back to that night and make it up to you. He's going to give you your Sophomore Frolic only this time, he's going to be your date."

"But why would he do that?"

"Because he probably loves you," Kristine said in a matter-of-fact tone. "Guys only do things like that when they're in love."

Lana and Meggie both looked at their assistant manager. Meggie had heard the same thing a hundred times from Lana, she'd even heard it direct from Dylan's lips, but coming from an objective observer, she couldn't help but wonder if it was true. "But how can I go? It's the grand opening of our shop. I can't just leave."

"Of course you can," Lana said. "Business is going to be slow for the first few days. Besides, this is more important than coffee. This is about a man."

Meggie stared at the dress, fingering the fabric. Dylan had to have gone to a lot of trouble to plan this evening. He couldn't have found her dress without her mother's complicity. And renting out the South Boston High School gymnasium probably didn't come cheap. And a limousine? She sighed softly. Though she didn't want to believe it, she had to agree with Lana. This looked suspiciously like a grand romantic gesture. "I guess I'll have to go out and find the perfect shade of pink nail polish before eight this evening," she murmured.

"Try it on," Lana said. "I want to see how it looks."

"It probably won't fit. I was really skinny back then. And flat as a board."

"Try it on," her partner insisted. She turned Meggie around and pushed her through the shop to the office. "If it doesn't fit we'll have to get it altered. I know a seamstress who could probably do that for you."

Reluctantly, she took the dress back to the office and closed the door. She slipped out of her Cuppa Joe's apron and shimmied out of the standard black pants and white polo shirt that made up the rest of the daytime uniform. The dress looked like it had just been cleaned and pressed and the crinolines scratched her legs as she pulled it up over her hips.

The strapless bodice made a bra unnecessary and Meggie twisted around to pull up the zipper. To her surprise, the dress fit. She smoothed her hands over her hips then turned and stared at the big bow sitting on her butt. "That's got to go," she murmured. "I'll wear the dress but there's no way I'm drawing that much attention to my nearly thirty-year-old backside." She grabbed scissors from the top desk drawer, then hurried back out into the shop.

When Lana and Kristine and Danielle saw her, they all stopped talking and stared. Meggie glanced down at herself. Except for the color and the big bow, she didn't think it looked that bad. "I know, I look like a big blob of cotton candy," Meggie said.

"You do not," Lana countered. "Actually, that dress looks better on you today than it did when you were a teenager. You fill it out rather nicely."

Meggie glanced down and noticed the considerable amount of cleavage showing. She tugged at the bodice of the dress, but it refused to rise any higher.

"I have the tackiest set of rhinestone earrings and choker at home," Kristine said. "I can run back to my apartment at lunchtime and get them."

"And you need gloves," Lana added. "Those long sexy gloves."

"And why not get me a tiara while you're at it," Meggie said. "So I can look really stupid."

"Meggie?"

The voice echoed through the empty shop and they all turned to see a customer standing near the end of the counter. Meggie stepped closer, then realized it wasn't just any customer, it was Olivia Farrell. "Olivia!" she cried. She hurried toward her, then tripped clumsily on the hem of her dress. Meggie caught herself by grabbing the edge of the counter. She straightened and smoothed the skirt of her gown, then yanked at the bodice again. She knew she must look like an absolute fool, but she was so happy to see Olivia again, it didn't matter.

"I'm so glad you came. So, what do you think?"

"It's wonderful!" Olivia said. "Very retro. You should have told me you were going for this look. I'll bet I could find you lots of really great deals on kitschy accessories. Really cool fifties and sixties stuff." She stopped and stared at Meggie, then shook her head. "I just have to ask."

"The dress?" Meggie said.

"It just doesn't go with the whole theme you've got going here."

Meggie giggled. "It's not supposed to. I was just trying it on." Olivia raised her eyebrow and Meggie quickly shook her head. "No, I'm not wearing this out in public."

"Then why are you wearing it at all?"

She hurried to the counter and grabbed the invitation then showed it to Olivia. "I think this is all Dylan's doing," Meggie said. "I think he plans to recreate that high school dance he was supposed to take me to."

A slow smile broke over Olivia's face. "So that's what he's been up to lately."

"What?"

"He's been asking me the most bizarre questions. And he was at the shop yesterday looking for—" Olivia stopped. "No, I'm not going to tell you. It should be a surprise."

"Why is he doing this?" Meggie asked.

"I'm sure he has a very good reason. But I wouldn't ask questions. I'd just have fun with it."

Meggie nodded. But her mind still whirled with the possibilities. Did this mean that he'd forgiven her? And where would they go from here? Or maybe this was just his way of putting things right before he moved on, she mused.

Whatever his motives, Meggie was certain that after tonight, her life would change forever.

DYLAN STOOD ON the sidewalk outside Cuppa Joe's. He glanced at his watch. "Seven fifty-five," he murmured.

Now that he was here, he wondered if he'd made a mistake. Perhaps he should have included an RSVP with the invitation. At least then, he'd know whether he'd gotten all dressed up for a reason. Dylan knew he looked stupid, but that was the whole point. He'd once heard Olivia say to Conor that she realized he she loved him when he'd rescued her cat, hissing and spitting, from her landlady, then drove miles with it tearing apart the interior of Dylan's Mustang. There was something about a man making a fool of himself that women found endearing.

To that end, he'd picked out the tackiest tuxedo he could find. It was an awful shade of burgundy with velvet ribbon trim on the lapels. The shirt was straight out of a seventies Vegas lounge act, all full of ruffles. He even found patent leather shoes in the same shade of burgundy, though he'd had to pay the formal wear shop extra to dig them out of the back of the storage room.

He leaned over and spoke to the chauffeur who was standing next to the limo. "I'll be back in just a minute."

Dylan straightened his velvet bow tie then stepped up to the door of the coffee shop, the small corsage box clutched in his left hand. The interior was dimly lit and he was grateful for that. But as he slowly walked to the counter, he realized that there were more than just a few customers watching him. Though he was happy for Meggie that her first day of business was successful, he couldn't help but be a little embarrassed for himself.

Lana stood at the end of the counter, a smug grin on her face. "You look...so silly," she said with a low giggle. She stepped up to him and gave him a hug. "I hope Meggie appreciates this."

"You like the suit?" Dylan asked. "I picked it out myself."

"Either you have really bad taste or you're willing to do just about anything to make Meggie happy."

"It's the latter, believe me."

"I'll go get her," Lana said. "She's hiding in the office."

"No," he said. "Let me."

He strode to the rear of the shop, then knocked softly on the door.

Meggie's voice came from within, muffled by the door. "Is the limo here?"

Dylan didn't answer. Instead, he knocked again. The office door swung open and Meggie stood in front of him, dressed in the pink gown he'd begged her mother to find. "Hi," he murmured. Dylan couldn't think of anything else to say. He knew the moment he saw her, every clever thing he'd planned would fly right out of his brain. He hadn't seen her in days and all he really wanted to do was stare at her. "You look beautiful."

Meggie smiled. "You look very handsome," she said.

"Are you ready to go?" he asked.

Meggie nodded and Dylan offered her his arm. They slowly strolled through the shop, their exit observed as closely as Dylan's entrance. When they reached the door a smattering of applause broke out and Meggie turned back and gave the customers a playful curtsy.

They settled themselves in the back seat of the limo and Meggie turned to him. "I was surprised when I got the invitation. After what happened the last time we—"

He reached out and pressed a finger to her lips, resisting the urge to pull her into his arms and kiss her. "That hasn't happened yet. Nothing that went on between us has happened. And some of it never will. We're starting over, going back to the beginning. We're going to do this the way it should have been done thirteen years ago." He handed her the corsage box. "These are for you."

A tiny smiled curled Meggie's lips. "You thought of everything, didn't you."

He helped her open the box then pulled out the flowers and slipped the elastic band around her gloved hand. The scent of gardenias wafted through the air. "Actually, this is a new experience for me," he said. "I never used to take dates to the high school dances. You're my first."

"I am?" Meggie asked.

Dylan nodded. "I could never afford it. But I've got a pretty good job now." He reached for the bottle of champagne that sat in an ice bucket on the opposite seat, then poured them both a glass. As they sipped at the bubbly, Dylan relaxed a bit. He'd been as nervous as a teenager getting ready for this date, wondering if he could make it work, if he could take them back to the very beginning.

He glanced over at Meggie. She sat silently, her champagne flute clutched in her fingers. Dylan had the whole evening planned for them, a perfectly timed agenda to make it the most romantic night of her life. But now that she was here, all he could think about was pulling her into his arms and kissing her. And that wasn't supposed to come until after...

He reached into his jacket pocket. "I was going to wait to do this," Dylan said. "But I can't wait. I want you to have this." He held out the huge ring emblazoned with the crest of South Boston High School.

Meggie stared at it for a long moment, stunned speechless by his sudden declaration. "It—it's your class ring," she murmured.

"Yeah," Dylan said, nodding. "Another first. I've never given it to a girl before, but I decided we should go steady."

Meggie giggled. "Steady?"

"Yeah. And you better say yes, because you have no idea what I went through to find that thing. I tore my father's house apart. I finally found it in the last box I opened in the attic."

"Steady," Meggie murmured. "What does that mean?"

"I means that we don't date anyone else. And it means that we spend all our free time together. And it means that you're my girl."

Her eyes shimmered with unshed tears and she put the ring on her finger. "That sounds good." A tiny giggle slipped from her throat. "It's a little big," she said.

Dylan held her hand up and examined the ring closely. "So it is."

"I suppose I could wrap yarn around it or wear it on a chain, like the other girls do."

"Or I could give you a ring that fits." He reached into his pocket and pulled out another ring, then held it out to her. Meggie's eyes went wide and she gasped softly. She tried to speak but her only reaction was a tear that trickled down her cheek. Dylan reached out and caught it with his thumb, then held her face in his palm and stared deeply into her eyes. "I know it's a little early. After all, we've only been going steady for a minute or two. But this ring will fit much better."

"Is this—" She paused. "Are you—" A sigh came with her next breath. "But we've only known each other—well, we've known each other for sixteen years. But we've really only known each other for a few weeks."

He took the ring and pressed it into her palm, then gently wrapped her fingers around it. "Whenever you're ready, Meggie, you just let me know and I'll put that ring on your finger."

Meggie nodded, then pressed her fist to her chest. They

gazed at each other for a long time, Dylan taking in the details of her face, the way the dim light shone off her hair and the way her lips looked so perfectly kissable. "I love you, Meggie. I said it once, but I didn't say it right. I think I've been waiting my whole life for you and you were there the whole time, waiting for me. I just didn't see it. But I promise that for the rest of our lives, I'll never take my eyes off you."

Meggie took a ragged breath, then blinked back more tears. "I used to dream about a moment like this," she said. "I had this whole fantasy worked out in my mind of how it would be. But I never imagined it this way...this perfect." She reached up and smoothed her palm over his cheek. "I love you, Dylan. Not a silly schoolgirl love, but a real love that I know will last forever. I loved the boy you were and now I love the man you became."

Dylan leaned forward and brushed his lips against hers. But it had been so long since he'd kissed her that he couldn't stop there. He pulled her into his arms and lost himself in the taste of her. This was the woman he wanted to spend his life loving and he felt like the luckiest man in the world to have found her. He drew back and gazed down into her eyes. "So I guess my plan worked."

Meggie smiled. "You had a plan?"

"I even wrote it down. And there's much more to it," he said as the limo pulled to a stop in front of the school. "Just wait. You're going to love this."

The chauffeur opened the door and Dylan stepped out, then held his hand out for Meggie. They walked to the front entrance of the school where a janitor waited to open the door for them. Meggie stopped the moment they were inside then looked around at the dimly lit hallway. "I haven't been back here since I graduated. But there's something about the smell of high school that you never forget."

Dylan pulled her along toward the gym. The double doors were open wide and a single light from above illuminated a small table set with a catered dinner. Soft music drifted from a boom box nearby. He reached over and flipped a light switch and the entire ceiling came alive with tiny twinkling lights.

Meggie gasped at the sight, then turned to him. "How did you do this?"

"It's a secret," Dylan said. In truth, it hadn't been as hard as he thought it would be. The school was closed for the Thanksgiving weekend. A deal was struck and the boys from the Boylston Street fire station put their ladder skills to work. Tomorrow morning, they'd be back to take the lights down.

"So, can I have this dance, Meggie Flanagan?" Dylan asked.

Meggie turned to him, then threw her arms around his neck and pressed a kiss to his lips. "You can have this dance and all the other dances for the rest of my life." With that, she pulled him along to the middle of the floor, her skirts rustling against his legs. And when they stepped into each other's arms, Dylan knew it was perfect.

This was what love was supposed to be. And as he gazed down at her, the twinkling lights from above glittering in her eyes, her lips still damp from his kisses, he made a vow to thank his lucky stars every day for the rest of his life. He'd cast aside the tales of the Mighty Quinns and believed that love was possible. And then he'd found Meggie.

There would be a new Mighty Quinn tale to tell his children. About the way Dylan Quinn wooed Meggie Flanagan, with a pretty pink gown and an awful burgundy tuxedo and a diamond ring that he'd someday slip onto her finger. And as time passed, the story would become a favorite that he'd tell over and over, about how true love had made a Mighty Quinn the happiest man in the world.

THE TINY STONE church was lit by hundreds of candles, casting a magical light over the evening ceremony. Meggie sat next to Dylan in one of the old wooden pews, holding his hand and listening as the minister spoke about the eternal power of love, the words as meaningful to her as they were to Conor and Olivia.

Only family and close friends had been invited to attend the Friday evening ceremony held in a small village on the coast of Maine. The church was still decorated from Thanksgiving service with beautiful cornucopias on the old altar. And Olivia had chosen to fill the rest of the space with flowers in deep jewel tones that complemented the harvest colors.

They'd all driven up that morning, Meggie and Dylan, along with Brendan, Sean, Brian and Liam. Even Seamus had grudgingly agreed to attend although he was still trying to convince Conor of the danger of his actions right up until the start of the ceremony. The family had taken over a small inn on a bluff overlooking the Atlantic.

Though Meggie had only known Olivia a short time, the ceremony was exactly what she would have expected from her future sister-in-law—sophisticated, low-key, elegant. She wore a stunning dress, a strapless sheath that showed off her perfect figure and a simple fingertip veil. And Conor looked like all the other Quinn brothers, stunningly handsome in their tuxedos. Meggie couldn't help but remember the tux that Dylan had worn the night of the "Sophomore Frolic." In truth, she thought he'd looked even more handsome that night, so determined to right the past and give them a new future. But then, her opinion of that tux had been swayed by the man who wore it so convincingly—the man who'd asked her to marry him.

She'd been carrying the ring around since the night he'd given it to her, waiting for the right time to accept his proposal. She'd thought that time would come later, after they'd celebrated Conor and Olivia's wedding, when they'd retired to their huge room at the inn and snuggled up in front of a roaring fire. But now, as Conor and Olivia were pledging their love to each other, she glanced up at Dylan to find him looking down at her.

His eyes told her everything she needed to know. He loved her and that love was deep and lasting. And someday, they would stand in front of friends and family and pledge their lives to each other. Suddenly, Meggie wanted that life together to begin now.

As the sound of the minister's voice echoed through the tiny church, it was as if his words were meant not for Conor and Olivia, but for Dylan and Meggie. Dylan pulled her hand up to his lips and pressed a kiss to her wrist. And at that instant, Meggie knew the time was right. She pulled her hand away and then reached into her purse and withdrew the ring. She held it out to him.

They both stared at the twinkling diamond for a long moment. Then with a steady hand, Dylan took it from her. There was no need for words. They knew the pledge they were making was from their hearts. Dylan held the ring on the end of Meggie's finger and then looked into her eyes. She nodded, tears blurring her vision. Yes, she would marry him and yes, she would promise to love him forever.

As the ring slid down her finger and found its place, the minister pronounced Conor and Olivia husband and wife. But as they kissed, there were two people that didn't bother to watch. For Dylan and Meggie were caught up in their own private world, where nothing else mattered but the love they shared and the love they'd pledged to keep—a love that would someday become the stuff of old Irish legends.

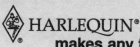

Celebrate the season with

Midnight Clear

A holiday anthology featuring
a classic Christmas story from
New York Times bestselling author

Debbie Macomber

Plus a brand-new *Morgan's Mercenaries* story
from *USA Today* bestselling author

Lindsay McKenna

And a brand-new *Twins on the Doorstep* story
from national bestselling author

Stella Bagwell

Available at your favorite retail outlets in November 2001!

Silhouette®

Where love comes alive™

Visit Silhouette at www.eHarlequin.com

PSMC

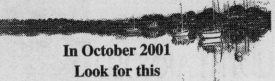

In October 2001
Look for this
New York Times bestselling author

BARBARA DELINSKY

in

Bronze Mystique

The only men in Sasha's life lived between the covers
of her bestselling romances. She wrote about passionate,
loving heroes, but no such man existed...til Doug Donohue
rescued Sasha the night her motorcycle crashed.

AND award-winning Harlequin Intrigue author

GAYLE WILSON

in

Secrets in Silence

This fantastic 2-in-1 collection will be on sale October 2001.

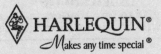

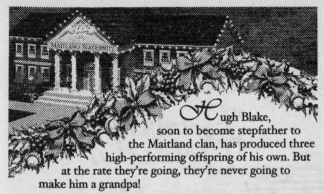

*H*ugh Blake,
soon to become stepfather to
the Maitland clan, has produced three
high-performing offspring of his own. But
at the rate they're going, they're never going to
make him a grandpa!

There's *Suzanne*, a work-obsessed CEO whose Christmas spirit could use a little topping up....

And *Thomas*, a lawyer whose ability to hold on to the woman he loves is evaporating by the minute....

And *Diane*, a teacher so dedicated to her teenage students she hasn't noticed she's put her own life on hold.

But there's a Christmas wake-up call in store
for the Blake siblings. Love *and* Christmas miracles
are in store for all three!

Maitland Maternity Christmas

A collection from three of Harlequin's favorite authors

Muriel Jensen
Judy Christenberry
&Tina Leonard

Look for it in November 2001.

Together for the first time in one Collector's Edition!

New York Times bestselling authors

Barbara Delinsky

Catherine Coulter

Linda Howard

Forever Yours

A special trade-size volume containing three complete novels that showcase the passion, imagination and stunning power that these talented authors are famous for.

Coming to your favorite retail outlet in December 2001.